A MEDICAL MYSTERY

THE IMPOSTOR

A MEDICAL MYSTERY

THE
IMPOSTOR

PAMELA TRIOLO

The Impostor

Pamela Triolo

F I R S T   E D I T I O N

HARDCOVER ISBN: 978-1-939288-83-7
eBook ISBN: 978-1-939288-82-0

PAPERBACK ISBN: 978-1-939288-81-3
Library of Congress Control Number: 2014950383

POST OAK
AN IMPRINT OF WYATT-MACKENZIE

Published by Post Oak, An Imprint of Wyatt-MacKenzie
postoak@wyattmackenzie.com

Praise for Triolo's *Death Without Cause*

"Triolo has masterfully woven a gripping mystery deep within the health care system . . . A true page turner." Gwen Sherwood, Author and Co-Editor of *Quality and Safety in Nursing* and books on *Reflective Practice*

"Pamela Triolo, debut mystery author, has penned a hit with her first book!" Eleanor Sullivan, Author of *Cover Her Body* and *Graven Images*, the Monika Everhardt Medical Mystery Series and other books

"The detailed description of the almost nameless antagonist and the warm and realistic depiction of the protagonist provide for a page-turning novel that forces one to read right up to the epilogue and leaves us hoping for more!" Sally Hartwig, Amazon Review

"Fast going, exquisite attention to medical detail and engaging characters make *Death Without Cause* a winner." Sharon D'Orsie, Amazon Review

"Her writing is cinematic . . . It's not often that a book grabs you from the get-go and doesn't let go until the end. This is one of those books." Dina Colman, Author, *Four Quadrant Living: Making Healthy Living Your New Way of Life*

"*Death Without Cause* is a page turner that holds the reader's attention from beginning to end. Her characters are interesting and realistic, compassionate and intelligent. For the layman, the story is enlightening and for the healthcare professional, especially nurses, it is a story to make us proud." Ann McKennis, Amazon Review

"Pamela Triolo's in depth of knowledge of nursing and hospitals shows as she carefully crafts the technical and interpersonal challenges of solving this mystery ... Her characters are realistic and personable and you care very much about them and the victims." Cindy Wigglesworth, Author of *SQ 21: The Twenty-One Skills of Spiritual Intelligence*

"This novel was refreshing as it intertwined accurate and current health care issues with an intriguing and plausible plot. Unlike some medical mysteries that tend to be full of inaccuracies as well as overly dramatic, Triolo was spot on with crisis scenarios that were crafted amid an exciting storyline." Krista Bragg, Amazon Review

"In addition to a riveting storyline, this book provides interesting insight into the inner workings of a hospital critical care unit ... The plot is chilling and makes you wonder if something like this could actually happen. A compelling read for a widespread audience and very impressive for a debut novel." Florence Osmund, Author of *Red Clover, Daughters, The Coach House*

"Triolo's deft characterizations make her an author to watch." Kirkus Reviews

For my dearest father and mother,
who provided for and challenged me.
Thank you for everything.

"Dates of destiny are always on time."

Anonymous

STACI

"In the middle of this road we call our life
I found myself in a dark wood with no clear path
through."
Dante Alighieri, *Divine Comedy, Inferno*

The dingy highway motel room reeked of a sordid past. The storytellers lingered: cigarette smoke, the musty smell of mold, greasy pizza cardboard, and the sickly sweet odor of death. The ancient window air conditioner rattled and wheezed like the diesel engine of a pickup. Sweat trickled down Staci's back. She needed a shower, badly. First she had work to do.

She sat at the battered desk in the dimly lit room, cheap vinyl curtains drawn to block prying eyes. She glanced at her reflection in the mirror above the desk. A young woman stared back, fine features overpowered by a cascade of dirty blonde curls. Green eyes flecked with amber appraised the image in the mirror. She tilted her head to the side and pulled back the curls, securing them with a black scrunchie. High cheekbones and a full mouth emerged, completing the heart-shaped face. She peered closer and gently touched her hairline. A fresh bruise lurked there, purple and yellow, a grim reminder of the choices she had made.

Methodically, she removed everything from the woman's wallet. She carefully laid the contents on the worn desk: credit cards . . . useless . . . she would not touch them. She counted fifty-eight dollars in bills with some change and then saw a traveling nurse agency ID card. *There might be something here.* An idea began to form. Over the years, survival had always meant having a way out. She had to be prepared to run when her world collapsed. Her mind worked rapidly, calculating potential scenarios. She continued to sort through the cards. Then, like being dealt a full house, she pulled out a Texas driver's license, an RN license, and—the jackpot—a social security card. When would people learn? She shook her head and smiled sadly.

The young woman had run out of gas on I-45 north of Houston on her way home from work on New Year's Eve. Staci and Cooper saw her and pulled over in front of her disabled car. He wanted to have some fun. Staci was reluctant but played along. He was constantly getting them into trouble. At twenty-five, he had the maturity of a high school jock kicked off the football team. Over a beer at a local ice house, she had fallen for his story—abusive father, dead mother. Staci couldn't resist his tousled brown hair, innocent blue eyes that would beg forgiveness, and a Southern drawl that made her insides melt like chocolate lava cake.

Cooper traveled from town to town working rodeos. He picked up extra money as a mule for a cocaine supplier out of Mexico. He lived out of a suitcase, in his truck or, when he had the cash, a motel room. Tonight, they were driving around looking for something to do when they spotted the car. They played the part of a couple of friendly good Samaritans. He had been drinking—too much. Staci and Cooper laughed and joked together, pretending they were on a date. Poor kid, she felt safe and got into their car. Then it went too far.

Staci drove. Cooper sat in the back with the nurse. He grabbed the woman, pulling her close, ripping her clothes and crushing her mouth with a kiss. Staci watched in the rearview mirror, disgust driving burning bile up her throat. He pulled out his knife. The nurse panicked. Her wide eyes, crying out with hope, briefly caught Staci's in the mirror. Staci looked away. She was driving fast, seventy miles an hour. The nurse opened the back door and rolled out on the highway.

Staci slammed on the brakes and pulled over to the shoulder.

"You bastard!" she screamed. "Look what you've done!"

Traffic rushed by, and the car rocked with the force of the gusts. Staci dashed out the door and ran back, searching for the woman. She found her crumpled on the side of the road. She knelt down and felt for a pulse under the jawline . . . nothing. Her heart sank. Lifeless green eyes, forever questioning, stared up at Staci. Dark black blood pooled on the road from the blonde's lethal head injury.

"How is she?" Cooper called, stumbling to the scene.

Staci glared up at him. "She's dead, you jerk."

"I'm going to be sick." He ran to the guardrail. She could hear him throwing up. Staci looked down at the young woman, and her mind rapidly created a plan to get them out of yet another situation. This one was a disaster.

"Get back here! We've got to move her . . . before someone stops."

"I can't."

"You will."

Staci stood up and walked over to Cooper. She planted both hands on his chest and roughly pushed him back. "You killed her!" She grabbed him by the arm and dragged him over to the body. "Nothing like this was *ever* supposed to happen."

"Well, it did!"

She held back what she really wanted to say. It wasn't the time. It *was* time to ditch this pretty boy before he landed both of them in jail. They half-dragged, half-lifted the body to the car as the late-night traffic blew by.

That was hours ago, and a lot had happened since then. A lifetime had happened.

They'd managed to heave the women into the trunk, bagging the battered head to minimize the blood trail. Then before dawn, they drove to a secluded patch of grazing land outside of Spring, Texas, carried the body far off the road, and buried the nurse where she would not be found for months, maybe years.

"Mary S. Stevens" was her name. Staci cringed at the thought of calling herself Mary. The last Mary she knew was during a stay in the second . . . no, fourth . . . foster home. After thinking for a moment, she decided that the middle initial and the green eyes were a perfect match for her plan—meant to be. *Isn't that called "kismet"?* "Staci Stevens" would suit her just fine.

Staci paused, glanced over her left shoulder, and took a long look at the still form of her partner of five months. His story had attracted her, a kindred spirit. She had felt sorry for him, wanted to help him out. Besides, he was cute. He had been fun, for a while. She'd hoped he might be different from the rest of the guys she attracted—a string of losers. She was wrong. First he'd started talking down to her. Then she could do nothing right. Then he started flirting outrageously with any female, regardless of shape, size, or age. She was certain he was sleeping around. But the last straw was tonight, when he hit her.

"What is it with me?" she said to the sad image in the mirror. "Why do I always attract the wrong guys?" She paused, looking into the eyes in the mirror. Fear pulsed up from her gut, and her heart pounded as dark memories of Blake surfaced. Like a fool, she had fallen for him. She'd believed that the raging river of their chemistry was love. *How many girls mistake chemistry for love?* She had been lucky to get away.

Her heart was troubled, heavy with remorse and regret.

"Twenty-three. I'm twenty-three, and what do I have?" It was time for a New Year's resolution she would actually keep. She continued to talk to the mirror. "Something's got to change. Something's got to give. I can't live like this anymore." She glanced back at his body on the bed. *What a mess.*

The plan that came together was risky, but she didn't have a choice. Cooper had paid a week's rent in cash. She removed his wallet, found the hidden wad of cash from his drug sales in his boots, and then destroyed all clues to his identity. She decided to wipe down the room for prints. She'd seen that done in movies. Take away any trace of her. She would have to wait to shower. Move on quickly. She would leave him here. Put a "do not disturb" sign on the door.

Got to move. Now!

SANTOS

United Flight 1138 streaked east across the snow-dusted salt-and-pepper plains of Colorado. With a cruising altitude of thirty-four thousand feet, clear skies and visibility well over ten miles, the flight crew settled in for a smooth ride into Houston.

In the cabin of the Boeing 737, Santos Rosa, RN, slept. Dressed in faded jeans, white cotton blouse, green suede jacket, and hiking boots, she might have been a college student returning from a stolen mid-semester ski week. The sun streamed through the window and splashed across her lap, warming her. Her thick mane of auburn hair, streaked with gold, cascaded to her shoulders. Briefly, she opened her eyes, readjusted the backpack under the seat in front of her, and checked her watch, a treasured possession of her late mother. Every time she looked at it she felt close to her—a physical connection with a beautiful soul she could no longer touch. It was a bittersweet feeling of comfort. The devastation of her loss was no longer razor sharp, but it still weighed on her heart. She looked at the watch again and settled back to find a comfortable position to continue her nap.

An announcement broke the relative quiet of the cabin.

"We have a medical emergency," reported a flight attendant, the steady voice pitched high with anxiety. "Do we have any medical personnel on board? Please come to galley in the back of the plane."

Instantly alert, Santos unbuckled her seat belt and

stood up. "I'm a nurse. Please let me through."

The two men in her row stepped out into the aisle.

Santos appeared younger than her twenty-six years, partially because of her size, a petite five feet. A seasoned critical care nurse, she was proud to be heading back to work in the Coronary Care Unit of the Medical Center Hospital, located in the largest medical center in the world, the Texas Medical Center. This nonprofit mecca for health care, the largest employer in Houston, employed over one hundred thousand people in some fifty-four member institutions that included hospitals, clinics, research centers, colleges, and universities. Working in the TMC offered Santos tremendous opportunities to learn and serve. Clinicians, patients, teachers, and students from all over the world sought the TMC for its reputation, cutting-edge research, and state-of-the-art patient care. She felt honored and blessed to be part of a great team of clinicians.

Santos walked quickly toward the galley, balancing on the seat backs, when sudden turbulence caused the plane to shudder. A large man lay sprawled on the floor, half of his body in the galley, legs in the aisle. Two flight attendants, a man and a woman, had removed the cushions from one of the seats and attempted to support his head.

Dropping to the floor to get a look at the man, she told the flight crew, "I'm a nurse."

"Thank you for responding." Santo heard relief in the voice of the young flight attendant.

"What happened?" Santos asked while assessing the man, who was struggling to regain consciousness. Her brain rapidly went through an automatic checklist, scanning for diagnostic clues.

"He came back here and just fainted."

Santos sat on her heels, at eye level with the patient,

and looked into his eyes. They stared back at her, unseeing.

"Here's the blood-pressure cuff and stethoscope from the medical kit."

Santos broke open the plastic lock on the zippered bag and removed the equipment. "It's not going to be easy to hear his heartbeat with the noise of the plane. I'm going to have to go by what I see on the dial." She put the stethoscope around her neck and then wrapped the cuff around the man's large arm. It hardly fit. He looked up at her, confused. As she inflated the cuff, he looked down at his arm. She got a blood-pressure reading—low. Sweat trickled down the side of his face. The flight attendant passed her a wet towel, and Santos used it to wipe his face, hoping to revive him further. She spoke to him calmly, her voice warm with professional concern, willing him to lock onto her voice and pull himself out of his stupor.

"I'm a nurse. My name is Santos. Are you diabetic?"

"No, no!" he responded shaking his head vehemently.

Santos breathed a sigh of relief. He was coming back.

"Will you need medications from the medication kit? The AED is right behind you," offered the lead flight attendant.

"No," Santos responded as she continued to assess his blood pressure. "I think he's coming back—should be fine if we can keep him awake."

The man looked at Santos, confused.

"Are you hypertensive?"

He nodded yes.

"Can you look at me? Follow my finger?" Santos looked in his eyes. He was tracking the movement of her finger. He was waking up now. That was good.

"What's your name?"

"Wayne."

"Where are you from, Wayne?"

"Louisiana . . ."

"Did you take your blood pressure medication today?"

"Three-thirty this morning . . . with a water pill."

"Can you tell me what happened just now?"

Embarrassed, he said, "I felt light-headed . . . then I thought I was going to throw up. I didn't want to do that, so I headed back here."

He was a big man, and his striped shirt was unbuttoned where one of the attendants had attempted to loosen his clothing.

"Can we give him a little breathing room, folks?" The hovering crowd stepped back. "Have you been drinking fluids today?"

"No." He looked back at her. She nodded, expecting that response. "You didn't want to have to go to the bathroom."

"That's right," he said with a nod.

"When you travel, and after you take your blood pressure medication, you need to eat and drink. You can get dehydrated." The words spilled out before she realized he would not remember a word she said. He was barely conscious.

She looked up at the flight attendant. "Do you have some water?"

The flight attendant passed Santos orange juice.

"Could I have water instead? It will be easier on his stomach—with a straw please?" Santos smiled. "Thanks so much."

"No problem." The flight attendant looked relieved that her passenger was waking up. She went back into the galley and returned with a cup of water and a straw.

"Would you like some of this?" Santos asked him.

"You need to drink, drink, drink when you fly." She smiled at him. "This air is so dry, it'll quickly dehydrate you."

He nodded. She held the plastic cup while he gratefully sipped.

"Do you need on-the-ground medical advice?" the senior flight attendant asked behind her.

"No, I think we're good here," responded Santos, her eyes never leaving her patient, relieved that he was reviving. "Mild dehydration—fluids should get him back to normal. Can you give him extra water until we land? Any chance you have some crackers or something to settle his stomach?"

"Sure thing."

Santos got up off of her knees and said, "Let's get him in a seat here in the back of the plane," then paused for affirmation from the crew. Together they guided the man, now fully conscious, to a vacant seat.

"You'll be okay," she said with a reassuring smile. "Try to get something to eat when you get off the plane." He nodded, looking exhausted and confused. "And check in with your doctor or nurse practitioner right away. Okay?"

"The captain has decided to speed up our return to Houston," the lead flight attendant said behind Santos. "I'll make an announcement when we land asking the passengers to wait until we can get our patient off the plane. The captain has decided EMTs will meet us. Can you accompany the patient off the plane?"

"Sure." Santos nodded and headed back to her seat.

Once settled, she pulled out Jodi Picoult's new book. She had heard Jodi speak at The John Cooper School Signatures Author Series, a fundraiser for the school and a platform for local authors. Santos loved the feel of books, turning the pages, the smell of the print. Her love of books began when her mother would take her to the public library as a child. The library had a distinctive smell—dust and ink. She could get lost in a book and her world would go away. She could walk side by side with fascinating characters she would never meet in worlds she might never see. She could travel back in time to Victorian Paris and see the clothes and homes of the characters as well as look deeply inside their hearts and lives. There was an intimacy in books that was often lacking in conversation.

At the end of a chapter, she put the book down and reminisced about the recent trip to Denver. This flight might be the last few moments of quiet for a long time. The American Association of Critical Care Nurses national conference had been great—in so many ways. Every year, her zeal for learning was fed by the conference speakers and the new colleagues she met. It was reassuring that many of the nurses faced the same issues she did. Over the years, Santos had developed a national network.

She'd even been able to catch up with Yasmin Kazan, a colleague and dear friend, who was doing a yearlong leadership exchange in Denver. They talked so much they hardly ate a bite. Leaving Yasmin behind was bittersweet—the Houston Ballet's Nutcracker Market would not be the same without her friend. She would have to take a hiatus from the annual tradition this year—unless her new neighbor, Lynne, wanted to go. Maybe even Mrs. Banks? They both knew each other from the neighborhood. That would be fun.

Reenergized, Santos was excited to return to work. She missed her colleagues in Houston, one in particular. She had loaded her backpack with a ton of professional material to share—more tools for the toolbox. As the time flew by in Denver, she kept in touch with nurses on the unit as well as her sister, Camilla, one of her six siblings, who had e-mailed to say they had planned another family dinner for Sunday. Count on Camilla, whose family lived in the Heights—a boutique community of wonderful homes and unique shops—to hold the family together after the death of their mother. Santos was anxious to see her father and especially *Abuelita,* her grandmother. Though Colorado had great Tex-Mex food, there was nothing like homemade family specialties, recipes passed down for generations in a family that had immigrated to the United States from Mexico decades ago.

Santos settled back in her seat and looked out the window at the expansive green forest emerging below. The plane was making its final approach into George Bush Intercontinental Airport. *Home. Patrick.*

She smiled and felt warm all over. Patrick Sullivan, RN, was five years her senior and a seasoned clinician in the CCU. Over the past few months, they'd been developing a relationship outside of work. Colleagues for several years, they were now taking their friendship into unknown territory. She loved him dearly as a friend, and they both hoped for something more. Regardless of what happened to them as a couple, she would be forever grateful to him. Since last year—the murders, the violence—fear seemed to hover, always a shadow on the periphery, darkening her life. Every day was a step further away from what had happened. And every day, her feelings for Patrick burned brighter. Was he the one?

Her emotions fluctuated from day to day, fueled by his obvious love yet confused by her fears. She couldn't put a finger on it—was it fear of being hurt, commitment, loss of control? His deep blue eyes, always sparkling with a hint of mischief, seemed to look right through her, reading her innermost thoughts, touching her soul. His kisses left her breathless. Her heart beat rapidly as she thought about it. She was frightened by how he swept her away. She needed to talk to someone, but she wasn't sure who—talking it out always helped to understand her feelings. With Yasmin gone, she was at a loss for a close woman friend. Emma? Camilla was always a possibility, but she was so busy with her family.

Valentine's Day was coming up, and they had talked about a special dinner. He would plan this date, she would plan the next. She smiled, and a sense of peace settled over her. She could just take this one day at a time. She looked down at the ground rushing up to meet the plane. Though Colorado was spectacular, this was home. It was good to be back.

BLAKE

"Evil begins when you begin to treat people as things."
Terry Pratchett, *I Shall Wear Midnight*

Blake Jarvis sat in a dark corner of the popular Fort Worth country-and-western bar, sipping a cold beer, watching the door. Shadows hid his dark, rugged features. It was Friday night happy hour, and business was brisk. Clusters of women entered the dim, boisterous interior of the rustic, wood-beamed bar, hung with Texas flags and those of the Confederacy. Big & Rich's "Save a Horse" played loudly in the background. With one finger, Blake tilted his hat, rocked back in his chair, stretched out his long, blue-jeaned legs, and smiled in anticipation. He had picked the right place.

He favored blondes and was always careful. He didn't want to pick them up too young. Daddy might have a curfew or be waiting up for them. It was best to pick a working woman, someone who lived alone. He liked to watch for a while. He savored the foreplay of the hunt—check them out and try to figure out if they were there to party with the girls, flirt with the guys, or potentially hook up. Reading body language was a challenge, and it made the hunting fun. It had been a while since his last conquest, and he was obsessed with finding the next object of his desire. Sex with a stranger was as common to him as beer with a burger. He was ravenous for a fix of creamy, soft skin with a touch of damsel in distress. Their fear was an aphrodisiac.

A tall blonde with short, curly hair, dressed in a trim

tan business suit, telltale briefcase in hand, stood in the doorway. Light surrounded her slim silhouette, and at first, he could not see her face. She hesitated as if trying to make a decision, looked around, and headed for an empty seat at the bar. She sat down, dropped her briefcase on the floor, leaned in to the bartender, and ordered. Her clothes marked her as new—out of place in a bar where jeans and boots were the uniform of the night.

He sauntered toward the bar, weaving through the tables, eyes always on the prize.

"Buy you a drink?" His lips curled into a movie-star smile. He knew he had a powerful impact on women. Freshly showered, he had put on aftershave—not too much, just a touch. Every detail of his appearance was calculated, designed to attract, to set a lonely girl's heart throbbing.

She turned around and politely smiled back. He watched as her blue eyes, lush with dark lashes, first looked at his mouth, then traveled to his dark brown eyes, and finally rested on his thick, curly black hair. He held his hat in his hand, waiting for the full impact to register.

She paused, thinking.

"Thanks, but no thanks . . . I just stopped by for a drink on the way back to my hotel."

His mind raced ahead to the possibilities and pleasures of corralling this independent filly in a hotel.

"Come on, Darlin' . . . one drink. Don't break my heart." He crossed his hat across his heart.

She looked down and considered.

"One drink?" he asked again. "Can't you see I'm lonely?"

She shook her head. "I'm sorry, but I have work to do tonight. One drink is my limit." She smiled at him like he was an annoying child and pushed back from the bar.

"I've got to go."

Dismissed, turned down, the rage of rejection rippled through him, and he stood his ground, blocking her way. His jaw tightened, and the smile froze on his face.

"I've got to go," she repeated firmly and glanced back at the bartender.

He took a deep breath to calm himself. The bartender stood watching.

Best to back off. Not make a scene.

"Maybe next time," Blake said, his smile relaxing. He gallantly swept his hat to the side with a flourish, clearing the path for her to leave.

She picked up her briefcase and with a nod to the bartender, headed to the door. He watched her leave. His hands balled into fists, and he opened and closed his fingers, trying to control the anger that threatened to explode in his chest while considering what he would have, could have done with her.

Bitch! Just another blonde bitch . . .

So much like the one he'd lost.

The one he was looking for.

Where was she?

SANTOS

The next day Santos drove into Houston for a family dinner at Camilla's. She had packed a small suitcase and planned to spend the night at Camilla's and make the easy drive to work in the morning. Though she hated leaving a week's worth of mail piled on her kitchen counter, an overflowing laundry basket, and a garden that looked like a jungle, family dinners were rare and a priority. The chores would be there when she returned home the next night.

She was excited to see everyone. Since it was Sunday, she had dressed up in a short black suede skirt, boots, a cream silk blouse, and a new red vest she had found at a Western boutique in the Denver airport. Blessed by light traffic, she made the trip from Spring to the Heights quickly.

Santos drove up to the Craftsman-style home, a Sears catalogue model built in the early 1900s. A wide screened-in porch spanned the front of the house. Lush, green Boston ferns punctuated the expansive seating area. Cozy wicker rocking chairs lined with colorful pillows tempted family and guests to linger. Many a lazy hour was spent here reading, daydreaming, or playing games, sipping tall glasses of iced tea or lemonade.

Over the past month, Camilla's husband, Miguel, had built a treehouse in the gigantic burr oak out back. Evidently it could hold a card table and chairs or sleep five in sleeping bags. Santos smiled with anticipation. Not only was she excited to catch up with her family and see the new treehouse, but she was starving.

She noticed a silver Jeep parked down the street. *Patrick?* No, it couldn't be. How would he know she'd be here? Her heart raced with the euphoria of new love, then fell when she realized it couldn't be his car. Santos gathered her purse and small bag and then locked her car.

"Hey you! Need some help?"

She looked up at the voice calling her from the porch.

It *was* Patrick. She smiled, and her heart filled with happiness when she saw his tall, lean form. She quickly crossed the street and ran up the short flight of stairs to the porch.

"I didn't know you would be here!" She dropped her purse in a chair and set her small suitcase on the porch.

"Camilla thought it would be fun to surprise you," Patrick said, smiling. His heart-melting sapphire eyes were dark with longing. He reached out for her. "Come here . . . give me a hug and a kiss before I lose you to the family."

Santos laughed, wrapped her arms around him, and stood on her toes, her lips parting for his kiss. The connection with his waiting mouth sent a shock wave of warmth down to her toes.

"I missed you," he said as he looked down at her. "I think it's harder on the one left behind. *You* were off having fun in Denver. Probably did some skiing too."

"I did *not* ski . . . no time," she said, chocolate brown eyes flashing gold sparks. "Don't be a pain so early. I just got back. I missed you too." She stopped to run her hand over the top of his head, feeling the rough cut of his buzz. "You cut this any shorter, I'm not going to be able to tell you're a blond."

"Keeps me cool. Makes cleanup after a run easy," he grinned.

"You look great," she smiled. "Every time we're apart,

I think of all of things I'd like to share with you."

"Me too," he said. His eyes twinkled. "So what are we waiting for?"

She pushed him away, laughing. "We just got started! We haven't even had our first Valentine's Day together!"

"Speaking of that, I need to talk with you about a couple of things before your family discovers you're here."

"Everything okay?" Santos's bright mood suddenly clouded with worry.

"Pretty much . . . just wanted you to know that Emma is going to be out for a while."

"Is she sick? Is she okay?" Emma meant the world to her. What would she do without Emma? She had been Santos's clinical mentor from the beginning. Emma was a linchpin, a vital member of the CCU team. Valued for more than her expertise, she was loved by her patients and the medical staff. Like Santos, she was also multilingual, fluent in both French and Creole. Santos felt blessed to be around Emma's compassion and intelligence. She hoped someday to have the poise and grace Emma demonstrated every day. Even on the most volatile days in the CCU, Emma's calm presence reassured everyone around her. Her down-to-earth advice and sense of humor helped make the most difficult situation easier to bear.

"No, she's fine, but her mother fell and broke her hip. She had to head to New Orleans to take care of her."

"Oh, I'm sorry. Is her mom going to be okay?" Santos's heart felt heavy with grief, remembering her mother's death. Now Emma might be going through the same thing.

"From what I know, she's just eighty, has always been healthy, and has a great spirit . . . so her recovery chances are very good."

"That's a relief, but I'll really miss Emma. She's a rock,

such a great mentor. Will she be gone long?"

"Don't know. I'm sure we'll find out more tomorrow from Heather. Believe me, I'm going to miss her too—maybe not for all of the same reasons *you* do."

"I know." Santos laughed, and her worries fell away. "She *feeds* you . . . and Nick. You're both going to be out of luck now. Nick's going to die when he hears this news. He's going to fade away to nothing."

Emma was generous with her fabulous Creole cooking, bringing extra from home several times a week. Nick, tall and lean as a flagpole, was one of the cardiology residents and a good friend of Patrick's. He had the metabolism of a hummingbird and the nose of a beagle. He could track food from floors away. A hungry staff member who was lucky enough to get to the fridge before Nick could usually find something to warm for a quick stand-up lunch or dinner break.

"Guess so," Patrick said, shaking his head. He brightened, "Unless you start cooking more for us. That would be great!" His smile beamed, proud at his great idea. He took both of her hands and looked down at her with adoring eyes that pleaded for food.

He was hard to resist.

"I'll see what I can do." She rolled her eyes and sighed. "We might need to organize potlucks for the unit more regularly. Okay, Patrick, so that's the bad news. Do you have any good news?"

"Of course! I've been researching restaurants for Valentine's Day. There's a relatively new one in Bellaire—Costa Brava Bistro. It's Spanish and French food. I went over and checked it out, even picked out a table for us."

"That sounds great. We don't get much time to try new places."

"Can you stay overnight with Camilla that night . . . so you don't have to drive back to Spring?" He smiled and then looked serious. "Or you could spend the night with me."

"You're moving too fast." Santos stepped away from him. The front door opened, flooding the porch with light. Spanish and English spilled out into the cool night air.

"Santos, you *are* here!"

"Papa, yes, just arrived." Santos reached for her father, burrowing her head into his shoulder, smelling the comforting scent of soap and Old Spice. He held her close. *Perfect timing. Saved by my father!* She felt such peace enveloped in the safety of his loving arms. Though she knew he was happy to see her, when she looked up at him she saw grief lingering in his eyes. His shoulders drooped, and his eyes began to fill with tears.

"You look more and more like her."

"I'll consider that a compliment, an honor." She smiled and hugged him again.

Camilla's generous frame filled the doorway. Her lustrous, long black hair, parted down the middle, was pulled back into a bun. Her light chocolate skin glowed from the warmth of the kitchen. She wore a beautiful, vintage cream jacquard blouse and red flared skirt; a long black silk cord with a silver cross hung from her neck.

"Is the party out here?" She gestured wide with her arms.

"Camilla, no, I just arrived, and we were coming in." Santos rushed over to give her older sister a hug. Camilla smelled like enchiladas and felt like home. "Thanks for doing this again."

"Mamá would have wanted it this way," Camilla replied.

"I know," Santos replied. "I miss her terribly."

Camilla smiled and nodded. Her eyes were shiny with tears.

"Oh, before we get going in there—come upstairs with me for a minute. I have something for you." Hands on her hips, she teased, "Patrick, can I drag her away from you for a minute?"

"Si Camilla . . . es tuya!"

"Working on your Spanish, Patrick?"

He grinned. "Trying . . ."

"Keep working!" Camilla laughed and turned to Santos. "Come on Santos, quickly."

"When do I get to see the treehouse?" Santos asked.

"Later, later . . . after dinner."

Santos spied Abuelita, her mother's mother, tucked away in her usual corner. She always seemed cold and had acquired a collection of shawls. Today she wore a beautiful hand-woven turquoise shawl. Her gray hair, pulled back into a neat bun—her signature style—accentuated her slim face and high cheekbones. She was a classic beauty. Santos gave her a quick wave. Abuelita responded with a smile and blew her a kiss. They would catch up in a minute.

Camilla led the way up the creaking, mission-style oak staircase.

"Gorgeous blouse," Santos remarked as she followed.

"Got it at an estate sale, antique tablecloth material," Camilla responded. "It turned out pretty good, don't you think?"

"Can you make me one someday?"

Camilla nodded, walked into the master bedroom, and headed for the closet. She emerged carrying a pair of beautiful brown-and-black leather Lucchese boots.

"You probably recognize these," Camilla began. "I don't wear them, and I think Mamá would want me to give them to you." She held the boots out to Santos.

Santos reached out and fingered the intricately tooled and gently worn leather. Overcome by emotion, she could not speak. Tears stung her eyes.

"They're an heirloom, and they should be worn and cherished. Mother will live on with you when you wear these boots." Camilla spoke seriously. "And someday, when you have a daughter, you will pass them on to her . . . a gift from the grandmother she will never know." Camilla's voice broke.

Santos reached out to hug Camilla. For a moment, the two sisters were silent, suspended in time, sharing unspoken memories.

Santos finally found her voice. "It has been such a year of loss."

"I know, Honey, but loss makes us appreciate the happy times . . . treasure them. Loss is a part of the tapestry of life. Without the little nubs and imperfections in the pattern, we wouldn't appreciate the joys in life."

Santos nodded. "Thank you, Camilla. Can I wear them now? Do you think Papa will mind?"

"Of course not. He'll love seeing you in them."

Santos sat on the edge of the bed, pulled off her boots, and put on her mother's. She stood up and looked down. "Oh, they fit perfectly. They're gorgeous! I forgot how beautiful they were." Santos smiled at Camilla. "Thank you so much. I will cherish these always."

"Mom! Mom! Mom! Where are you?" Six-year-old Alfonso's voice floated up the stairs accompanied by the pounding of little feet. "Can I eat in the treehouse?"

Camilla broke away. "We're coming," Camilla shouted in the direction of the stairs. "No, you will eat with family!" She shook her head and muttered, "Never a dull moment around here." Camilla sighed. "Santos, if you want to take a quick look, you can see the treehouse from this window."

Santos parted the curtain to look out. "Wow!" escaped from her lips. The treehouse was some twenty feet up, nestled in the huge, gnarled branches of the ancient burr oak. It looked as if the tree was holding the little house in its arms. It was multileveled to fit into the tree limbs and surrounded by wood rails. Painted white, the little perch in the sky had a brown shingled roof. A ladder entered the structure through a trapdoor in the center. A small red, white, and blue Texas flag hung from the front of the house. Childhood memories bubbled up, filling her with joy—tea parties and climbing trees, constructing makeshift tents, and sleeping under the stars.

"That is quite a treehouse . . . looks just like your house in miniature. That's amazing! Same shingles and everything."

"We'd better get down there; everyone's probably hungry."

"Let me help," replied Santos, and they headed down to join the boisterous crowd.

STACI

"Just when the caterpillar thought the world was over,
It became a butterfly."
English Proverb

Staci studied her metamorphosis in the full-length mirror. A stunning blonde with dark, bold eyebrows, intense hazel green eyes, and a stylish cap of curls stared back at her. She smiled, pleased with what she saw. The cut set off her high cheekbones, and the color did wonders for her looks. The past six weeks of hard work had prepared her for this capstone moment. The professional makeover, worth every penny, was the final step in her transformation.

Staci admired her body. She was tall, lean, and well proportioned. At least she had some redeeming qualities—the rest of her life had pretty much been a mess. Staci fingered a small scar in her abdomen, a lingering memory of a knife wound—another bad choice. Whatever had made her think she was so tough she could hang out with a gang and escape without a scratch?

She'd never known her parents. She'd grown up in foster homes, some good, some not so good. She'd met a few warm, loving foster parents who were hungry to give a new life to children. Yet her first sexual experience, an assault by one of her "brothers," had not only robbed her of virginity but of the hopes and dreams every young woman has about her first love—about life itself. It drained her self-esteem. She felt like trash and acted like it. Her desire for approval, for belonging, had led her into the arms of the wrong men.

She looked at the image in the mirror and shook her head, remembering. One wrong man topped them all—Blake. She had fallen hard, captivated by his charm, his dark good looks and fabulous body. His fantasy sex was fun at first, but when he . . .

Her chest tightened, and her heart beat faster as she remembered. The man was a sex addict with a taste for violence. He was insatiable. She looked into her own eyes and hugged her arms tightly across her breasts, shivering, cold with fear. He was a predator. She slipped on her robe and walked away from the memories that surfaced at the mirror.

She wanted so badly to take advantage of this opportunity, this new identity, and become someone different—not just on the outside but inside. Was that possible? Proud of her body, she'd always taken care of it, no smoking, no drugs, and alcohol only in moderation. Over the past few weeks, she'd started running and realized she was a natural. She buried her loneliness in a crust of armor—her physical strength. Finding the discipline to build strength and endurance translated into actually starting to like herself. She would be smarter now, more careful.

She had hoped that in her new life she could sleep without the loaded SIG Sauer P238 under her pillow. No way. The first time she tried, two weeks ago, she tossed and turned all night. She pushed her anxiety deep into her subconscious, but it surfaced in her dreams. Chased, she frantically searched for a place to hide. One night she woke up sobbing, huddled in the closet, her shelter as a child. She thought about all of the kids out there, victims of their pasts, suffering from the same PTSD that plagued the victims of war. She was one of those kids, a member of the silent epidemic of unspeakable childhood trauma. She did not feel safe enough to put away her gun, the one thing that had been her constant companion for years. In fact, it was the only consistent thing in her life.

Keeping true to her New Year's resolution, with Cooper's drug money, her stash of emergency cash, and money from waiting tables, she moved into a tiny but clean studio and found an accelerated EMT program. She knew she needed some background training and felt that EMT school would be logical and relatively fast. Time was not her friend. Who knew when Mary's body would be discovered?

She decided that applying in person might get her into school more quickly. She had never applied for anything before—not a credit card or a bank account. She dressed carefully in a conservative slacks and a long tapered tunic she bought at a consignment store. She found a purse at Goodwill for a dollar that was in great shape and still in style. She steadied her nerves and set up an appointment. The class was full. She went into action, eyes full of tears, telling the administrator about the recent death of her husband and her need to get into school in order to get a job. He fell for it, and she was in the next day.

She packed the month of January and early February with so much activity that she barely slept. Classes, studying late into the night, and gaining field experience took every waking moment, seven days a week. She picked up used nursing textbooks at Half Price Books and worked on medical terminology and the language of her new profession. She walked the halls of the UT School of Nursing and TWU, dressed the part of a student, picked up nursing journals in the lobby and student lounge, and read them from cover to cover. She sat in the common area in the

TMC and listened to the students talk, studied their speech nuances as well as watched their teachers—imprinting.

The next step, while still in EMT school, was applying at a traveling nursing agency—not Mary's. She had a little more confidence now. Tall, fit, and attractive, she could now walk the talk. She had acquired more clothes so that she would make a good first impression. She was in luck. The agency needed more critical care nurses, and her background as an EMT, as well as Mary's previous clinical background, served her well. They wanted her to take a tertiary level refresher course in CCU at Medical Center Hospital. What a break!

Working as an RN was more than a calculated risk. It was a triple threat. If caught, her worlds would collide. Practicing nursing without a license would result in criminal charges and land her in jail. The authorities could trace her connection to Cooper and charge her with manslaughter or even worse, murder. The clock was ticking on the elaborate illusion she had created. The thought of the consequences cast a constant shadow on her happiness. Was she ready for this challenge? Was the danger of discovery worth the risk? Could she stay in character, bury her past?

Now the EMT dress rehearsal was over. She created an electronic trigger for her throwaway phone that would alert her to news of the search for Mary or discovery of the body. Cooper's body had been found. The case had no leads— for now. Staci realized she probably didn't have much time in her new role, but she would let it ride as long as she could.

The agency had arranged for her to precept in the CCU with a great nurse, Emma Perrine, RN. This would be the crucial test. Would this nurse be able to see through her disguise? She had studied, prepped, and costumed for the role of a lifetime. Could this step redeem her soul? She would have to make certain that Emma was duped by the charade, blind to the con. She would use every street skill she had acquired in her short but long life to continue the deception.

She tried not to think about the repercussions if caught. Nothing could be worse than the life she had left behind. With all her heart, she wanted to start clean, fresh, do something right—be a part of something good for a change—scrub away the layers of dirt that were her past. Put it behind her. For once in her life, she had hope. Could she pull it off? Her new life depended on it.

HEATHER

"The best thing about the future is that it only
comes one day at a time."
Abraham Lincoln

Heather Lewis, PhD, RN, Unit Director, CCU, paced the empty conference room, alone with her thoughts. Staff would soon arrive for the multidisciplinary meeting, the first of many meetings today. She had two important topics to cover, and their gravity made her uncharacteristically anxious. Today she would launch some of the most important work of her career. Ironically, she was also facing the most daunting challenge of her personal life.

She had carefully chosen her costume—clothes and jewelry—to give her the energy and confidence she needed for this day. Her long brown hair, touched with gray, was swept up in an elegant French twist. She wore a royal blue blouse under her fresh white lab coat, hoping it would brighten her pale complexion. A small strand of pearls, a gift from Don after their first child was born, graced her long neck. The matching pearl earrings were an anniversary gift. She hoped that no one would pick up her feelings. She waited, placing a smile on her lips, silently praying that she would find the right words to say.

Santos and Patrick walked into the conference room, chatting away, oblivious to the world around them. They were in love. This was the beginning of their life. She smiled wistfully and reached up to finger the smooth strand of pearls, remembering. A lifetime ago . . . hearing her son's first cry . . . Don's eyes so full of love.

Heather had made fresh coffee and brought in apple-cinnamon coffee cake laced with creamy custard. It was still warm and fragrant from the oven. Patrick made a beeline for the treat. The avid runner was always hungry. She watched him and smiled. Baking was meditative. It kept her mind clear and focused, especially important now when her life was spinning out of control.

"Welcome back, Santos! How was the conference? We missed you." She gathered the petite nurse into her arms. Her heart was full of love. Santos hugged her back. Heather cared deeply about her team, yet guided them with high expectations.

"It was great. I've got lots of info to share. I'll post it on the unit website this week. Okay?"

"Sounds perfect."

"What do you hear from Emma? When is she coming back?"

"She's not sure. It all depends on how the family triage works out. She's hoping one of her sisters can relieve her in a month. It could be longer."

"A month! A month? We're really going to miss her."

"Yes, I know. We all are . . ." The conversation triggered a reminder. "Oh, Santos . . . later, after this meeting, I need to ask you to do something I was hoping Emma would do. We can talk later. Okay?"

"Sure, whenever you're ready. You know you can count on me."

Reassured by Santos's beaming face, Heather thought, *she's a treasure.*

Richard Whiting, MD, Unit Medical Director, entered the room with Melissa Bentley, a member of hospital legal counsel and chair of the ethics committee. They were deep in conversation. With effort, Heather turned her attention to the newcomers. *One step at a time . . . Take it one step at a time.*

Whiting finished his conversation with Melissa, smiled at Heather, and then saw Santos. "Santos, welcome back! How was the skiing?" His green eyes twinkled with mischief, and he ducked away from Santos and headed for coffee, his long white hair—a clue to his past—captured in a ponytail.

"I didn't have any time for skiing! You're going to get me in trouble!"

Whiting laughed and walked over to stand by Heather. She felt his warm, dry hand grip hers with a reassuring squeeze. She reciprocated, comforted by his presence. As the formal leaders of the team, they had shared much together, from traumatic events to many successes. She looked up at him and gave him the best smile she could manage. He nodded and their eyes met. She saw compassion and understanding. He leaned over to whisper, "You'll do great."

"Tell me about it! Of course you skied." Nick Landon, MD, Cardiology Resident teased Santos as he headed for the treats. The room was nearly full of staff—which meant it felt like a boisterous family gathering. "The weather was perfect for skiing. I checked it every day!"

"Nick, you'll pay for that," Santos said as her dark eyes flashed golden bolts. "What is this? A conspiracy?" The room was loud with conversation, and nobody bothered to answer her question.

Santos, desperate to change the subject, said "Kathleen, it's almost your one-year anniversary as a staff nurse, isn't it?"

"Close. It seems longer, with all that has happened

around here. It will be in May, right around Nurses Week."

"We need to celebrate," Santos said.

"Nick, what's going on with you and Nancy?" Patrick asked. "Did you check out Mother's—that bar I told you about?"

"Yeah—great setup with karaoke *and* live music. We could have some fun there sometime," Nick replied. "They just finished some remodeling. It looks great."

"I know the one you mean," Richard cut in. "The original owners named it after the bar in *Peter Gunn*. I jammed there with the one and only Rusty Jones of blues rock fame, years ago."

"For real?"

"For real," Richard replied.

"You're kidding me," Nick replied. "Awesome!"

Heather looked at Richard, smiled, and shook her head. Hard to believe this man, a successful cardiologist with an impressive track record of innovative research and publications to match, was a former college dropout and studio musician. He had left college and hitched to LA with his backpack and a dream. He made it big then met his future wife—who had no intention of going on the road with him. Richard was a classic example of how people mature differently and everyone has a story.

Heather waited a moment longer. Most of the staff had arrived, a family with a purpose. Every day they shook off their aches and pains, their issues and worries, and launched into the mission of serving others. Doing a great job in the CCU required sacrifice, focus, and commitment. Lives depended on them. Her heart warmed and then grew sad as she thought about how much she loved her work family.

She took a deep breath, steadying her nerves. "Let's

get started, everyone. Grab some coffee and a seat, we've got work to do . . . let's go."

The room quieted as everyone settled in. Heather began, "We usually run this meeting with two staff co-chairs, and we'll get to that in a moment. Richard and I wanted to talk with you all about a very important task force we want to launch . . . and then another matter." She cleared her throat and looked at Richard for reassurance. He winked.

"We'll begin with the task force. We have the opportunity to change health care in a remarkable way, not just in our unit, but perhaps across the country." Heads nodded. She continued, speaking slowly, weighing every word.

"In our society, we spend a great deal of time planning for important life events. And there is a great deal of support in our culture for *most* life events. For example, engaged couples plan for marriage with their family and friends, their church. There are bridal showers and bachelor parties. There is a ritual around getting ready to have a baby. The new parents go to class, practice breathing exercises—train for labor. We create and decorate the new baby's room. Baby showers usually help support the couple and welcome the new child. But there is one very important life event that we rarely plan for—the end of life."

She looked around the room for understanding and immediately felt validated—the group was hooked.

"Since you are all experienced clinicians, you've seen your share of unsuccessful codes: CPR with not only chest compression, but defibrillation on the elderly or when there is no hope of survival—when most of us knew that from the beginning, but for whatever reason, we couldn't get a DNR. CPR with hope is by nature traumatic, emotionally and physically. CPR without hope could be considered unnecessarily violent, abusive, and a waste of resources, both human and financial."

Richard leaned in to the group to continue the thread of the conversation. "It's difficult for many families to face the fact that their loved one is dying or will never recover to a good state of health. Denial is a very strong coping mechanism. And many families, as well as the person who is dying, do not realize that they have choices. They have choices about *where* they die—at home with hospice, hospice care inside a hospital or in a freestanding hospice, an assisted living facility. The best place to die—for most people—is not usually the hospital."

"The cost of dying in a hospital is tremendous," Melissa added. "The centers for Medicare and Medicaid Services estimate that more than 25 percent of Medicare spending goes toward the 5 percent of beneficiaries who die each year. Twenty-five percent of the Medicare dollars are spent on 5 percent of people."

Kathleen Florence spoke up. "What really hurts me is the suffering we see . . . the unnecessary suffering—when there's no hope or when the patient hasn't made up their mind about what they want—the ET tubes, CPR when there's no hope, ventilators that can prolong life when there is no chance of the patient ever regaining consciousness. Just think of how of patients complain of being 'stuck' for blood, and the bruising you see that never heals."

The dialogue was going well, but it was time, and Heather circled the discussion back to the work ahead. "We can change this in our unit . . . even if we only have a few people every month who agree to begin the conversation about planning for the end of life."

Santos raised her hand and spoke up. "I saw the American Nurses Association position statement on DNR orders and Allow Natural Death decisions. Is that what we are talking about here? The purpose of the statement was to minimize unwanted treatment and unnecessary suffering. Is that where you're going with this?"

"Yes," Heather responded, happy that the team was taking the topic and running with it. "Glad you are reading, Santos."

"I saw somewhere . . . maybe CDC data . . . that for people over sixty-five, only about 25 percent die at home, and 50 percent die in the hospital—that's awful. We should be able to do something about that. I hope I don't die in the hospital . . . not that I don't love ya'll, but you can come visit me at home."

Santos's comment triggered a few nervous laughs. Heads nodded around the room. Heather's guard fell and her thoughts strayed to her situation. Anxiety seeped into her consciousness, and her palms started to sweat. She could be facing this sooner than she ever dreamed possible. She shook off worries around the uncertainty of the future and focused on the work at hand.

"We're approaching this a little differently than many hospitals," Heather explained. "Elaine felt that by taking a grassroots approach—coming from clinicians at the point of care and patients—we might identify more families who want different options. Sometimes, referring a patient to a palliative care service can miss patients. Some clinicians don't believe in palliative care, so we have clinician bias. The way we see this program, every patient we have will have this conversation—not necessarily as a part of their original assessment, but somewhere during their hospitalization."

"We feel," Richard continued, "that this team is the perfect group to begin to design a task force, composed of people here and other experts we need, to create multiple pathways for the end of life that are customized to the patient and family, that are humane, and that provide the essential support for the end of life without prolonging suffering."

"We really need to get patient feedback—in sort of a focus group format—about how ready they are for this," Patrick commented.

"You're right," Heather replied. "We'll need quite a varied group to plan and design not just a guide for this crucial conversation, but the path to the best place for each patient to pass as peacefully as possible out of this life. And for each person, that path will be different. We'll have to create a template, a set of policies and procedures or checklists, that isn't too cumbersome or bogging our work down. Our goal will be consistent care that can flex with the needs of individual patients."

Santo's face showed a combination of reflection and grief—reminding Heather that Santos had only recently lost her own mother. "This is amazing!" Santos said, her voice trembling a little. "It could transform health care. It makes my heart ache just thinking about the people we've lost here who probably should have been at home or in hospice. There's some research out there about this and definitely a lot of discussion in the literature, but I don't know of any hospital yet that has done this."

"I'm sure someone has," replied Heather. "We need to find them and learn from them and develop the best practice for our patients and our community." She paused for a moment to switch gears. "Most of you may not realize this, but Emma has been through ELNEC training—we probably should identify who else in the hospital has attended these courses."

"What's ELNEC?" Nick asked.

"Sorry, Nick. ELNEC stands for End of Life Nursing Education Consortium. Its purpose is to improve palliative care by giving nurses in all specialties extensive education."

"We really have to help patients see that death is not necessarily a medical failure—and that not all clinical issues are curable," Nick added.

"And that death need not be violent . . . and that patients do have choices," Heather said. It felt good to see how quickly the team was jumping in and embracing the work. Their passion for patients and desire to be the best touched her heart.

Whiting continued, "We have so many end-stage cardiac disease patients that come in and out of the ER and the CCU who might be better served at home or in another setting. Today, chronic heart failure is the number one hospital diagnosis for patients over sixty-five."

"I didn't know that," injected Kathleen.

"It's true. In addition, the cause of death for 25 percent of the population is heart disease. And 50 percent of the people diagnosed die in five years, but that doesn't have to happen in the hospital. We have wonderful alternative care settings and telemedicine opportunities, some as simple as setting up FaceTime on the phone with your patients to check in on them or using something like Skype."

Heather stepped in again, already knowing the answer to her question. "Okay, so we have agreement this is important?"

"Yes," was the resounding response.

She smiled. "We need the task force to do two primary things: develop the guide for the conversation and then create multiple pathways for a peaceful passing where the patient and family have made informed choices. Got it?"

Heads nodded. "Moving right along, we need task force co-chairs, two disciplines . . . and be sure you cover all areas in the composition of the group—spiritual, clinical, psychological, social services, etc. Melissa is here because she is a member of our legal counsel and chair of the ethics committee. She'll help us with anything we need. Very likely we'll need to start with the living will of each patient."

"Welcome to the team, Melissa," Santos said. "It'll be great to officially work with you." She turned to the group. "Melissa has saved my you-know-what a number of times, giving me advice on ethical issues and helping me have the right kinds of conversations with some of the more difficult members of our medical staff. In my experience, you can talk to her about anything and she won't judge."

"Thank you, Santos," Melissa replied. "I'm really happy to be in the trenches with all of you. I'll help any way I can."

Whiting advised, "You will need to track the metrics, be prepared to defend your recommendations, and after a while, present and publish your findings to share with others."

"And by all means," Heather said, smiling, "include in the group some seasoned members. We can't have a group of twenty-somethings just talking to our patients about dying—you won't be credible. And you need to get patient and family input. We need to create paths that partner with them."

"Do we have volunteers to lead?" Richard asked.

Santos's hand shot up. "I will. After my experience with Mother's death, at home with hospice, I can tell you there is a better way than dying here."

"Great, Santos, thank you for speaking up," Heather replied.

"Why don't we call the project 'Pathways'?" Santos looked around the room and saw nods and smiles. "There should be no stigma attached to that."

"Great idea, Santos. Do we have a co-chair from another discipline?"

"I'll keep her in line," Nick offered. Santos rolled her eyes at Nick and then narrowed them to a glare. He missed her sparring look and continued, "My grandfather told me about something called Smart911. Evidently, it's a program that some communities have adopted. It allows you to sign up and actually create an online profile of your medications, medical conditions, disabilities—even pets. Most people can be pretty upset when they call 911, or even unable to talk. If you call from the phone registered in the Smart911 database, it can alert first responders of unique conditions and wishes—to stop CPR at home or any other kind of treatment, if you don't want it."

"That sounds great," Kathleen said.

"I've heard of it," Melissa said. "I don't think I've seen it in Houston. How old is your grandfather?"

"He's ninety and healthy, but he does not want to be resuscitated. He's had a good life, and spiritually, he's at peace."

"Sounds like he has the right attitude," Melissa replied.

"Nick, you and Santos will be a good match—you'll complement each other," Richard said.

"I'm excited," Heather continued. "I think you will make a great difference for our patients, beginning in this unit and hopefully spreading through our hospital, and perhaps further." She looked down at her notes and switched subjects, aware that the tide of excited conversation had temporarily buried her discomfort around what she still had to say.

"One more housekeeping detail before we have a conversation about something else. As a Magnet hospital, you know we don't use traveling nurses anymore. We don't need them. We have virtually no RN vacancies. But while we don't use travelers, they are important in other hospitals and can be lifesavers. One of the solid agencies has asked us to provide critical care training for one of their nurses, and Richard and I have agreed. We'll try it and see how it works out. Please give her your support. Her name is Staci Stevens, and she'll be joining us in a week or so."

Heather paused for a moment to look around the group. The dreaded moment had arrived. There was nothing else to say—no way to avoid the situation that had preoccupied and burdened her thoughts for weeks.

"This next topic is difficult for me, and I'm going to ask you to let me get through this quickly. I'm not able to answer a lot of questions right now." She looked at Richard, sitting across from her. He nodded and smiled as if to say, "You can do this."

"Some of you may have noticed that I've been in and out of work recently. I didn't want to say anything until I knew for sure . . . but I know now." She paused to take a deep breath. "I've been diagnosed with breast cancer. It has progressed to my lymph nodes, and though my lumpectomies are finished, I need to start chemotherapy and then radiation."

"Ohhhh," escaped from Kathleen Florence's lips. She covered her mouth with her hands, and then looked down.

"Please, let me continue," Heather said softly. She didn't dare make eye contact with the group. Her composure was crumbling. "I've decided that the best thing for me, and the unit, would be to take a leave of absence and put someone else in charge." She felt the tension rise in the group as they waited. "If Emma was here, I would put her in charge in a minute. I know that would be the easiest on all of you. But she isn't here, so we have to bring someone in from the outside." She paused and took another deep breath. "There is a nurse, an experienced manager who has applied for a position with our hospital, but we have no director positions available. After talking with Elaine Schilling, our chief nursing executive, and Richard, we have decided to give her the opportunity to lead this unit in my absence. Her name is Sandra Bane."

Hands shot up, and Richard stepped in. "Folks, we aren't prepared to answer a lot of questions right now. Be assured, I'll be here, the team will be the same, and when Heather is better, she'll be back. Those are the givens we know now. By this afternoon, I'll post on the unit bulletin board a schedule of check-in meetings. They'll be weekly, but short. I realize this is hard on you—on all of us—but we have patients to care for, we have work to do, and it's my hope that when Heather returns, you'll have great progress to show on our new task force."

Heather nodded, letting conviction steady her voice enough to raise it and gain the attention of the group again. "Before we end this meeting, I have a couple of things I need to say. I chose not to hide this from you—to spend my energy healing, not hiding. Most of you know I'm a private person, but I've opened my heart and home to you." She paused and smiled. "I have a wonderful coach, Roberta, who has given me great advice on boundaries and communication. I ask that you not ask me how I am. If I want to talk about how I feel or what's going on, I will bring it up. Otherwise, I want to focus on surrendering to the process, taking it a day at a time, and before you know it, I'll be finished and back with you. Elaine has been wonderfully supportive, and my leave is open ended. I can come back when I feel ready."

She looked over at Richard and nodded. She was done. It was done. Time to surrender.

"Meeting's over, folks," Richard said. "I'm happy to talk with anyone, anytime, but our focus has to be on patient care. I'm sure that Heather will welcome your prayers."

She managed a small smile and fought back tears, exhausted from the effort. She couldn't bring herself to meet anyone else's eyes. "I'll miss you guys, but I'll be back!" she said. Her throat choked with emotion.

"Thank you, everyone. Back to work." Richard held open the door to the conference room, ushering everyone out.

"Santos . . . Santos," Heather called quietly. "Could you stay for a moment?"

Santos walked back to Heather. The room had cleared and they were alone.

"I told you that I needed you to do something for me," Heather began.

"Yes, anything. What do you need?"

"I would have asked Emma to precept the agency nurse, but she's not here. This young woman needs orientation and introduction to the rest of the team. Will you do it?"

Heather made the mistake of looking into Santos's eyes as she asked the question. Santos's eyes spoke the truth—the fear that was in her heart. Heather saw deep sorrow—like she was dying. It made her feel as if she was alive at her own funeral. *I'm not dead yet. I can't take this.*

"Santos, please don't look at me like I'm dying.

I'm not."

How could she ask Santos not to look so scared and hurt? Santos's mother's recent death and the string of deaths in the CCU reminded Heather that the team was very vulnerable—and now this. She already struggled to manage the duality of her work life with the new and unknown challenges she faced as a patient. Working while well was a challenge. Working while under treatment for cancer would compound that challenge. Heather knew she would have to learn to ask for help.

"I'm sorry. I don't know what to say . . . right now."

Santos brushed a tear aside and nodded.

"Will you orient Staci? Show her the ropes? Give her feedback? And ask for help when you need it."

"Of course."

"Thank you, Santos," Heather smiled weakly. "Everything is going to be all right. Please *try* not to worry." Heather hoped her words were an affirmation—designed to both reassure herself and Santos.

This was going to be tough.

SANTOS

Santos left the conference room feeling crushed and sad. For more than a year, the deaths of people she loved and patients she cared about had haunted her. Heather had taught her so much and knew her so well—almost like a mother. She felt off balance. She was losing the rocks of support in her life. When would this cycle of pain end? *Does a year ever go by that's quiet and peaceful?*

Kathleen and Patrick stood talking in the hall in front of a long wall of windows that overlooked a garden atrium. As they talked, they were looking outside. The spring wind had picked up, ominous billows of dark clouds towered overhead, and droplets of rain pelted the windows. Trees and shrubs bent with the wind.

Santos took a deep breath, let it out, and joined them. She looked out over the pale green promise of spring as it received a drenching dose of much needed rain. Glancing sideways, she noticed that Kathleen appeared to have been crying. Kathleen turned to Santos and threw herself into her arms.

"I can't believe this! After all we've been through, now this!"

"Shhh ... shhh ... quiet now," Santos whispered softly, putting her feelings aside for the younger nurse. "Heather will be out in a moment. You don't want her to see you this way."

Kathleen nodded, her eyes bright with tears. Patrick passed her a handkerchief, and Kathleen wiped her eyes and blew her nose. "I'll get this back to you, Patrick—clean!"

Her voice steadied a little. "Patrick, you must be the only guy on the planet who still carries handkerchiefs." She managed a smile, and they shared a quiet laugh.

"Comes in handy," Patrick said and looked directly at Santos. Her heart remembered and warmed. She smiled back at him.

Santos put her arm around Kathleen's shoulders, and the three nurses walked down the hall.

Santos spoke calmly and in a low voice. "We can't expect Heather to console us. She's got too much going on as it is."

"What we can do is hold the place together, launch the task force, and do what she would expect us to do," Patrick chimed in. "Nose to the grindstone."

"We can give her our prayers." Santos stopped. An idea popped into her head. "I know what you could do, Kathleen, if you have the energy. It's something very important and really helps people who are grieving. And believe me, Heather is grieving right now—she has lost one of life's most important blessings—good health."

"What? What can I do? I feel so helpless right now."

Santos faced Kathleen and placed both hands on the younger nurse's shoulders. "When my mother was dying, she had a friend, Ginny. Every week, something would come in the mail from Ginny. Either a card or a small gift." Santos looked up at Patrick and smiled. "She would even send Papa cards, sometimes with a prayer card, sometimes a tiny journal, but every week, without fail, they would get something from Ginny. It meant so much to them."

"People often send one card or note and feel they have done their part," Patrick put in. "What was it about Ginny that she knew what grieving people really need?"

"I asked Ginny some months after Mother died, 'How

did you know that's what they needed? How did you know it would be so appreciated?'" Santos's eyes filled with tears, but she continued. "Ginny told me that over twenty years ago, she had a son. That son died when he was eighteen months old. Can you imagine losing a child? How much that would hurt, forever?" She paused to look at Patrick again. He nodded soberly, and his blue eyes turned dark with concern. "When Ginny came back from her leave, she had a hole in her heart. But everyone thought she was fine . . . because she was back at work. She'd received the usual amount of sympathy cards and flowers, but once she got back to work, no one talked about it anymore. No one realized that she was still suffering terribly."

"She learned that people need comfort all the way along the path? Not just at the beginning or the end?" Kathleen responded.

"Yes, exactly. And learning that changed her life and the way she responded to people's pain and the difficult times in life. She *so* comforted my parents. You have no idea how much. Papa still talks about her to this day—how she made them feel remembered."

Kathleen stood up straighter. "So what can I do?"

"Well," Santos smiled, "why don't you work on organizing a . . . sort of . . . stream of support for Heather? Don't go overboard or push people to do something they don't want to do. But think of a series of things the staff could do, in a cycle that would give her a steady feeling of being remembered. I would stay off e-mail—send cheerful and inspirational cards via snail mail, or just sent handwritten notes. Cards signed by a group of people are always nice. Could you do that?"

"Yes, I can do that. It's a perfect job for me. I won't feel so powerless."

"Great. Think about it. We'll help you get it together, but I need you to take the lead," Santos replied, "because I got another assignment from Heather."

"What's that?" Patrick asked.

"She wants me to orient the traveler—since Emma is away." Santos thought better of speaking further in front of Kathleen. She felt a lot of concern about the task ahead. "Kathleen, why don't you head back to work, and we'll be there in a minute?"

"Got it," she said and turned back toward the unit.

"What's on your mind?" Patrick asked.

Santos frowned, torn between honoring Heather's request and being true to her beliefs. She chose her words carefully.

"Patrick, I have to tell you that I'm biased about travelers. I haven't worked with many, but I've read the research and heard rumors of their lack of commitment and poor skills. I hope I can keep an open mind with Staci."

"I understand, but it's something Elaine and Heather want us to do. I know you'll do great. If anyone can make sure the unit's safe, it's you precepting her. You'll be the best judge of her abilities. If she worries you or doesn't work out, then you need to talk it over with Richard—or Sandra."

Santos shook her head and sighed deeply. "We don't even know Sandra. I feel as if the place could be falling apart—no Emma, no Heather. Now we're two of the most senior people on the unit!"

"You know what they say," Patrick offered. "Education is no excuse for experience, and experience is no excuse for education. You'll get both. I'll be here. We'll grow together with the rest of the team."

"I'm really going to be busy," Santos continued, "orienting this new person, graduate school, and co-leading the task force with Nick." She bit her lip, considering how she would juggle the full plate of work and school.

"I'll help any way I can. You know that," Patrick smiled his reassurance and took her hand and squeezed.

"Thanks," she said. "It's just my initial response. I'll work through it."

"You're tougher than you look," he joked.

"You watch out!" She gave his arm a poke. She smiled as her mood lifted. "Changing subjects, I'm really looking forward to Valentine's Day."

"Me too. Time to get back to work."

Santos saluted, "Yes sir," and laughed.

SANDRA

"I saw a werewolf drink a piña colada at Trader Vic's
His hair was perfect."
Warren Zevon

Rain beat against the window in horizontal sheets, and flashes of lightning accompanied by rumbles of thunder interrupted the silence of the night. Sandra Bane laid alone in bed, wide awake in the darkness, hands behind her head, supercharged with an energy that was erotic with anticipation.

She was thrilled with the new opportunity. It was a virgin forest of possibilities. No one at MCH really knew her, and few would know her history. Her ability to charm, a string of professional degrees, and their desperate need, had opened the door.

After all, it was her right to rule. She was smarter than most, calculated and clever. She never stopped thinking. Passed over and put aside at her last hospital, it was time to move on to new territory. They were so stupid. Her rage, always on simmer, flared. Didn't they know she would do anything to get results? It didn't matter what. Not having a conscience made that easy. Yet they put her in a box.

Her brilliant mind worked in hyper-drive. How to shape-shift, then integrate into the culture—create a new empire. How to deconstruct and then make it hers. She would do a lot of listening, learn about the staff, assess them—discover their hopes, dreams, and fears. Sure, there would be resistance—there always was—but there were ways to minimize, marginalize those who stood in her way. Her techniques were more stiletto than sword, elegant, swift, and silent.

She had discovered her potential for wielding power and the subsequent thrill while working as a college summer intern at one of the major energy companies in Houston. First, she used her body to make her way through the hungry men who populated the C-suite. She studied the men, how they garnered power and used it. Her youthful, adoring looks at their senior faces and aging bodies stoked their egos, and her discretion made her a favorite. She was privy to their secrets and mentored by many. She watched, listened, and learned. Her lust for power was voracious. Lack of a conscience compounded her potential.

She found the nursing part of her education to be demeaning but useful. The Houston area was flooded with hospital administration majors, but the clinical knowledge gave her an edge. The business and finance courses she took would give her the credibility for a management role.

Once out of college, with newfound knowledge not just gained from teachers and books, she deliberately created her signature look and style—the costume for her character. Far from beautiful, she made the most of her looks, beginning with a sculpted, professional appearance and clothes selected with assistance from a personal shopper. Routine Botox and Restylane injections with a fitness routine keep her appearance in check and her mind sharp. Her studies paid off, she was hired into management roles, developed expertise, and was highly valued for her ability to speak both the language of clinicians and administrators.

Though she had studied *The Princessa*, *The Art of War*, and other books, she could have written her own book on power and manipulation. This was not her dream job, but it was a great opportunity to practice her art—a major rung on the ladder she intended to climb to the top. She swallowed the bitterness of losing her last job and considered the possibilities fueled by rumors of realignment in MCH, a hospital in the works outside of the TMC, and new organizational charts. The leadership team was aging. There would be retirements and new positions. Her success in this entry-level position would be the first test of her abilities. And she would exceed their expectations.

She would construct a monster mesh of dynamic support at all levels: physicians, patients, staff, and administration. Divide and conquer her resisters. Drive the unit to success—her success.

She would begin with a comprehensive analysis of the unit—clinical, human, and financial. Interviews with staff would begin immediately. Simultaneously, she would review everything from staffing and scheduling to overtime use, budget, policies and procedures, and performance evaluations. It would be fun to mine the staff for information—their hopes, dreams, and what she would call "opportunities for improvement," but were really their weaknesses. The friendly interviews would invite disclosure of all kinds of secrets, including information about Heather and Richard—information she would use to power her success. Her craving, the calculated pursuit of power, was her obsession.

She would attempt to recruit an army of follows. Seduce them with praise, feed their poor self-esteem, and bind them to her with grateful loyalty. "Always tell me the truth," she would say. "I need the truth." Knowledge was power. Insight into their hopes, fears, and issues was ammunition.

It would be important to devise and execute a diversion. Get them to focus on something other than their new manager. What should that be? *This is so much fun!* She smiled in the darkness.

Sandra had no empathy for staff and therefore no capacity to care about them. Her lack of compassion left her unencumbered. Life was messy for others, not for her. It was easy to make the tough decisions. She cared only about how decisions furthered her success and career, not about what her decisions did to others. From budget cuts to layoffs, when something needed doing, the consequences to others never cluttered her mind or kept her awake at night.

She would protect her soft underbelly at all costs. Her suit of armor was an illusion, hiding a deep fear of criticism and failure. Keep the wall up, the illusion intact, achieve results, and she would be fine.

Sandra harbored a dark hope, dwelling on it like a mantra, willing it—that chemotherapy would destroy Heather, sideline her for months, perhaps damage her heart, crippling her with congestive heart failure or perhaps a viral infection that would attack her already immuno-compromised state, killing her. She wanted the unit for her fiefdom, not just now, forever.

SANTOS

Santos woke to the February sun streaming through the blinds. Work was tiring, physically and emotionally. Thankfully, she was off today. She lay in bed for a few minutes organizing her day. She had a lot to accomplish: preliminary task force work, a few errands to run, packing clothes, and then driving into Camilla's for late afternoon tea. And then there was dinner. She sat up in bed, excited and smiling.

It's Valentine's Day! What should I wear?

She slid out of bed, pulled on her long pale green cotton robe and slippers, and headed to her small kitchen—about two steps away from her bedroom. Santos lived in a small patio home with a great room, a galley kitchen separated from the living area by a small counter, and one bedroom. It was perfect for her, decorated with pottery she had collected over the years and colorful Kilim pillows on the sofa. Two of her mother's Impressionist landscapes hung on the walls, along with Tarkay prints. She admired the Israeli artist's work. He was one of the few artists whose consistent subjects were sophisticated women who always dressed smartly. The bright colors made her smile. Someday she might be able to afford something more than a print. Her mother had been a prolific and gifted painter, and Santos felt comforted by the beautiful oils with the distinct brushstrokes made by her hand.

In the kitchen, she ground beans for coffee. While it brewed, she opened the refrigerator hoping to find a piece of fruit to eat with her favorite whole-grain toast. She smiled. Abundance was fresh fruit in season. The refrigerator was loaded with fresh milk, juice, eggs, cheese, fruit, and vegetables. There was even a small glass container of homemade chicken soup. Mrs. Banks, her widowed neighbor, had stocked the refrigerator again. Over the past few months, Santos and Mrs. Banks had agreed on a trade of sorts. When Mrs. Banks went grocery shopping, she would also buy Santos's list. Santos would pay her for the groceries, give her some gas money, and help her with the heavier gardening chores. It worked out well for both of them. Mrs. Banks felt needed and useful and spared her back during gardening, and Santos saved time and always had fresh food in the house, no matter how busy work and travel kept her.

She put together her breakfast, set it on a small tray, and sat down at the kitchen table. She woke up her laptop, took a sip of coffee and a bite of crunchy toast, and started her research on death and dying, location for death, and current work in health care designed to make the end of life less traumatic. She started at www.NursingWorld.org, the ANA website, and clicked on the Ethics tab. Within an hour, she had sped through a dozen different hyperlinks from the US Department of Health and Human Services and the National Center for Health Statistics to the End of Life Nursing Education Consortium.

Her head spinning, she paused to look out the window at the beautiful day unfolding. She felt nearly overwhelmed by the abundance of information available. *Just one of the subtopics would be a great thesis for my graduate degree. This could be double duty—work and school.* In her usual fashion, she decided to organize her research into a three-ring notebook of reference materials. She would share the information with the new task force by posting the information and links on the unit's intranet website—no need for anyone else to have to start at the beginning.

They had decided the task force would be composed of the new graduate nurses, Kathleen Florence and Kamy Klein; Melissa Bentley from Legal; Mary Collins from Social Services; Chaplain Smith from Spiritual Care; and others as needed. Santos would add Emma when she returned, and they really needed Patrick's expertise. Richard Whiting would be their medical advisor and run interference with his medical colleagues—something he did often. She would also bring the traveler, Staci, on the team that she co-chaired with Nick. The task force would be a good opportunity for Staci to learn. It would also give Santos another occasion to observe Staci, assess her knowledge and values about end-of-life care, and simultaneously evaluate how she interacted with the team.

Santos printed up a ream of materials for her notebook and added information via hyperlink and PDFs to the intranet site. She looked up at the clock and saw with a shock that it was nearly noon. She quickly organized her materials, loaded her dirty dishes in the dishwasher, and rushed into her bedroom to pack and then take a shower.

PATRICK

"You know you're in love when
you can't fall asleep because
reality is finally better than your dreams."
Dr. Seuss

Valentine's Day had finally arrived. Patrick was both excited and anxious.

Our first Valentine's Day—the first of many?

He arrived early and walked into Costa Brava Bistro juggling a small wrapped gift and a cut-glass crystal bowl of red roses for their table. Entering the candlelit, quiet dining room, surrounded by bookcases and fine art from Spain, he felt as if he had entered the comfortable library of a private home. Delicious smells from the kitchen drifted into the room: saffron-scented risotto, meat grilling, and bread baking—universal comfort food. Co-owners Kitty and Angeles had carefully crafted a serene environment for their colorful palate of creative cuisine. Greeted by Angeles, Patrick was ushered to the table he had picked out weeks earlier, situated in a quiet corner.

"Happy with this table, Patrick?" she asked.

"Perfect!"

By 6:00 p.m., the restaurant was starting to fill with couples longing for a romantic, quiet evening away from home and work. The cozy setting was the perfect backdrop to put worries and responsibilities aside and focus on hopes, dreams, and creating new happy memories. He set the flowers in the center of the table, placed the Valentine's

Day card and gift at Santos's place, and waited.

As he looked around the room, he found himself with time to think. It was the first quiet moment in weeks. Doubts percolated up. Was the gift too intimate? Would she like it? Was he moving too fast? Was he in love with being in love? Was she truly the one?

He saw her as soon as she walked in the door. She was wearing an ivory knit dress with a long matching sweater coat. A long strand of pearls hung from her neck. She wore her hair up, and pearls dangled from her ears. *She is stunning.* His heart beat rapidly, and his doubts fell away as he stood to greet her.

She saw him and smiled. Her smile captivated him, tugging at his heart. It lit up her whole face. Her eyes sparkled. Her lips were glossy red, and her skin glowed. He felt dizzy.

"You're gorgeous," he said and leaned over to kiss her on the cheek.

"Well, thank you, sir," she said with a wide smile. "I clean up pretty good. Scrubs are not the most flattering clothes."

"I've never seen you with your hair up," he said as he guided her into her seat at the table.

"Decided since this was a special night, I would do something different—like it?"

She looked up at him smiling; her eyes were lustrous with happiness.

As he returned her smile, his heart spilled over with joy, and he knew for certain that his love was timeless. He wasn't in love with love. He was in love with Santos Rosa.

"Santos, you will always look beautiful to me—no matter what you do with your hair."

"Patrick, you're very kind . . . thank you."

Patrick took his seat and watched as Santos looked around and absorbed the soothing and beautiful atmosphere of the restaurant. "Patrick, this is so lovely—good choice!" She started to look at the menu and then noticed the flowers in the center of the table. "From you?" He nodded. She saw the card and gift and smiled. "You *are* a romantic—you really know how to make an evening special."

"Open it," he said.

"It's so pretty. Did you wrap it?"

"I confess, no. I'm not too good at wrapping gifts."

Santos sat for a moment admiring the small package wrapped in white tissue paper, sprinkled with tiny red hearts and tied with a red satin bow.

"Patrick, it's too pretty to open."

"Come on, Santos—I bought it for you. Besides, I'm dying to know if you like it."

She carefully opened the package and beamed up at him. "How did you know?"

"Know what?"

"That this is my perfume?"

Her tawny eyes were taking his breath away, making it hard to think. "I didn't . . . I didn't know. I just thought that perfume might be an appropriate Valentine's Day gift. I know you love chocolate. But I wanted you to have something you might wear and think of me . . . remember us and this evening."

"How did you find it?"

"Well, it was a little awkward. The salesperson kept recommending things, and I just asked if I could smell what they had. I tried out lots of perfumes. Then I smelled this, and it smelled like you. So I bought it."

"You're amazing!" She smiled and looked a long time at the perfume, placing the pretty red bow back on the box.

Then she opened the card. She read it, smiling, whispering the words. "Thank you, Patrick. You're the best."

She picked up her purse and pulled out a small, flat blue box with a red bow and a red envelope. She passed him the box.

"What's this?" he asked.

"Something you need." She smiled, and her eyes twinkled with mischief.

He untied the bow, opened the blue box, and started to laugh. "Handkerchiefs. You bought me linen handkerchiefs!"

"You're always saving us damsels in distress."

He connected with her smile, and she handed him a card. "And here's my first Valentine for you."

He opened up the card and read it. She had created a unique valentine for him with poetry from Kahlil Gibran's *The Prophet*. He read silently for a moment and then read out loud: "And think not you can direct the course of love, for love, if it finds you worthy, directs your course."

Touched by the words, he looked at the striking woman sitting across the table from him and said, "I'll keep it forever." She was so gorgeous, not only outwardly, but radiating an inner beauty. He didn't know how long his attraction to her had been growing—shaped by a thousand interactions at work, between them and with patients. She had a special magic with people—the ability to make them feel at ease, an empathy that was old soul in its wisdom. She was feisty and smart and best of all, his friend. He wanted to crush her in his arms, cover her red lips with his kisses. The longing was deep, and he struggled to keep it in check. He sat back in his chair, sighed to himself, and said, "Let's look over the menu. The food looks fabulous!"

Santos ordered the paella and Patrick the prix fix

menu. The bottle of rioja he had ordered arrived. Smiling, he lifted his glass. "Health and happiness . . . may this be the first of many."

"Health and happiness," she said, and they gently touched crystal glasses.

"Tastes wonderful," Santos said. "You're full of surprises, Patrick Sullivan."

"Just getting to know me . . . each other," he said. "Away from work."

The mention of work spurred her down that track.

"I wanted to tell you that I spent most of the day working on the Pathways task force."

He was hoping they wouldn't go there, but he could tell she was excited. She wanted to share. He would listen.

"There's a huge amount of literature on end of life, hospice, palliative care out there. I'm trying to get some of the research ready so we can have a preliminary PowerPoint presentation and get everyone up to speed. Heather told me I could use a section of our unit's website for posting information—to keep everyone current."

She stopped to take a sip of wine and then leaned across the table. "I think it's so sad that most Americans want to die at home, surrounded by their loved ones, but that rarely happens."

"I agree."

Santos stopped and looked down at her lap. She fiddled with her cloth napkin.

"What's wrong?"

She tilted her head to the side and looked at him sheepishly. "Not the greatest conversation for a romantic evening, is it?"

He laughed. She wouldn't be Santos without this earnestness, this passion for her work. "It's okay. We can talk about work for a while."

"You know," Santos shook her head, "you're going to have to help me learn how to have more fun."

That would be my pleasure, he thought. "It's easy to be serious, with the work we do, the situations we face—life and death every day. But I hear you. We can work on it together."

"Let's talk about Nick and Nancy . . . that's more romantic."

He smiled at that. He knew more about Nick and Nancy than he could share—he really wanted to, but Nick had sworn him to secrecy. But he could give her a hint. "I think they're getting close to taking the next step."

"Getting engaged? Already?"

"Well, when they finish their residencies, Nick wants to specialize in interventional cardiology, and that means a fellowship. I don't think he wants to be separated from her—even for a year. He's talking about Mass General, Dartmouth, Iowa."

"Wow . . . as much as he is a pain, I'll miss him."

"He's going to have to interview at all the places that might be interested in him. It's a lot of travel and expense, and exhausting to fit in with his work. Then, when he gets a match, Nancy will need to find a job on the anesthesia staff."

"Life doesn't get easier, does it? It gets more complicated, especially with two careers."

"Yes, it does, but two people together in life make life better." Patrick paused. "I've been thinking . . ."

"Oh—now what?"

"I've been thinking about our children, our honeymoon. I think we should go to the Italian Lakes—have you ever been there?"

"I've been thinking about our next date." Santos smiled and reached across the table to take his hand. "Shouldn't we slow it down a bit? How about dinner and a concert at Dosey Doe? Have you ever been there? I'll plan that date."

Patrick looked at the sincerity in Santos's chocolate-brown eyes. They were bright with happiness. His mother had reminded him that courtship was a dance—that if he really wanted Santos, he would have to lead sometimes and at other times follow. He felt as if this was taking an eternity. Then he remembered that sometimes going slow would get you where you wanted to go faster.

Santos smiled and shook her head. "Patrick, you're always thinking. Why don't we take our time? We have time, don't we?"

He wasn't sure how to put his feelings into words. "I think about your friend Carol, your mother, my father, and all the patients we've lost over the past year . . . and how sometimes, we think we have all of the time in the world, but we don't. How every moment is precious—like this moment now. It will never come back again."

Her eyes told him she understood. He saw the sadness that had been so constant lately, the depth that accompanied it. "I know. I watch the sunrise many days and know the sky will never, ever look the same again—the colors I see and the shapes of the clouds are forever changing, and if I don't stop to watch them, I will miss so much of the beauty in life."

"Like rainbows. If you don't look quickly, they're gone."

"I wonder how many beautiful moments we miss in life because we're so busy, rushing around, obsessed with work, our data phones, or the computer. It drives me crazy when I see families out together, all looking at their phones or on their phones. "

She looked around the room, then back at Patrick, and smiled. "It's so lovely here . . . thank you for this."

"You are welcome." He reached over to take her hand. She had managed to change the subject, veer the conversation away from them and onto life in general, and he hadn't missed that. But he needed to bring it back—needed to say more of what he felt. "I know that right now, you feel safe here . . . cocooned in this world." Patrick looked around the room, and Santos's eyes followed. "But it was just a few months ago that I nearly lost you."

Santos face turned pale with the memory.

"Life is fragile; our health is fragile—look at Heather. Cancer caught her completely by surprise."

"I know. One day she's just fine—and the next, she's having surgery and facing chemotherapy. I think of all of those people, including us, who go through life oblivious to the fact that things can change in an instant. When Carol went through chemotherapy for breast cancer, though she didn't talk about it much—she didn't want to scare me— the thing she missed the most was tasting food. She told me, 'You have no idea how much the taste of food means until you lose the sense of taste—or taste chemicals with every bite.'"

"That's sobering. And you're right. We need to be grateful, every day, for what we have, for our health." Patrick paused to take a sip of water. The conversation was slipping away again, but maybe it was best just to let it. Maybe the lines by Gibran were a sign. Love would direct their course.

He decided to go with the flow of the conversation. "By the way, I called Don yesterday just to give him support."

"How is he?"

"Devastated . . . worried. He feels powerless. I think he's a little depressed."

"I can understand." Santos paused for a moment. "Oh, I meant to tell you—Kathleen has created a plan—for the unit support system for Heather and Don. It's helped Kathleen feel like she's doing something. She's really excited. And she has the unit feeling like they can channel their love for Heather in meaningful ways."

"That's great. I need to remember to call Don on a regular basis, too."

Santos looked down at the table.

Patrick could sense that something was on her mind. "What's up? You can tell me."

"I really shouldn't bring this up, but . . . have you heard anything about him?"

Patrick could read the worry in her thoughts. "Hadrian?"

Santos nodded.

"Evidently his attorney is trying to plead innocence by reason of insanity."

"That's ridiculous . . . he deliberately . . ." Santos sputtered. Then she abruptly stopped and let go of his hand, sitting up straight in her chair. She looked around the restaurant at the couples deeply engaged in conversation and looked back, gazing deeply into Patrick's eyes. He saw warmth and love. For a moment he lost his ability to breathe again. She reached for his hand and squeezed. "Let's not invite him to our table tonight. Let's put the world away—all of our worries, the past. Let's be happy in this beautiful moment."

He took her hand and kissed the inside of her soft wrist. She smelled like roses.

"Well," he started, testing again, "let's talk about our future? Seriously, what do you think about a honeymoon in the lake region of northern Italy? Maybe Lake Como? I've wanted to go there for years. It's so beautiful, the combination of lake and mountains. You like mountains. I like water. Perfect—don't you think?"

"You mean you don't want to talk about the names of our children first?" Santos laughed. "The lakes are supposed to be beautiful." She smiled and looked deeply into his eyes. His heart nearly stopped. He wanted to drown in their honey-brown depths.

Anna, their server, arrived with their dinners and brought him back to reality. She smiled, looking back and forth between them. He started to breathe again.

"Such beautiful presentations! The food looks fabulous. I'm starving." Santos smiled. "Thank you, Patrick. I love you."

"Glad you're happy. You deserve to be happy. I love you too. And always will. No matter what."

SANTOS

Santos spent Valentine's night at Camilla's. The guest room was a cozy haven. The antique brass bed promised sweet dreams. Covered with a fluffy down comforter in a cream matelassé duvet, it was loaded with colorful embroidered pillows. Lavender wands from Provence infused the room with their soft scent, lulling her to sleep. Santos fell into bed and did not wake until the alarm jostled her back to reality.

She showered, dressed in her scrubs, and ran downstairs. The tantalizing smell of a hot breakfast drew her to the kitchen. Camilla, white apron tied around her ample waist, had been up for an hour. Freshly brewed hot coffee and warm croissants waited.

"I made you a latte this morning," Camilla said. "Thought the warm milk would be good in your coffee." Camilla looked at Santos and smiled, nodding. "I don't even have to ask about last night. You look dreamy with love—better wake up before you hit the CCU."

Santos laughed, and they chatted briefly about the restaurant and the evening. She took a sip of coffee and spread her flakey croissant with orange marmalade.

"Yum! I'm glad I don't live here. After a week I wouldn't fit into my clothes." Santos laughed and continued her staccato description of the evening. "They had chocolate sformato with amaretto whipped cream. It was so good. I'm going to have to make it for you someday. I've got to stop talking about food and eating. I gain weight just looking at food!" Camilla laughed, and Santos finished, "Maybe I need to take up running—another thing I can do with Patrick."

An hour later, Santos floated into work. The Valentine's Day dinner had been the stuff of great memories—it had exceeded her expectations and showed her a side of Patrick she had not seen before. Her heart was light, and she was warm with nostalgia—the rich currant taste of the wine, his warm breath on her neck, lips that swept her away. *Oh God, I'm in love!*

As she walked toward the central station in CCU, she noticed several clinicians gathered together. Patrick was leaning over the counter, and the sight of him made her heart skip a beat. As she approached, she noticed he was talking with one of the new graduates, Kamy Klein, who sat at the desk. Kamy's long dark hair, neatly plaited into braids, hung down to her waist. She already had a reputation for two things: her love of pistols and her affection for cowboy boots. Her boot collection rivaled Madonna's. Her maternal grandmother, a nurse, had immigrated to Houston from the Philippines. Her mother was also a nurse, and her father a cattle rancher—all of which made Kamy a typical Texan, born into a multicultural society. Her father had taught her how to shoot at age four. She was a walking gun encyclopedia. She always said what was on her mind, no sugarcoating, but was wonderful with patients. They all loved her.

Patrick held up a monitor strip, explaining something to Kamy and . . . *who was this?* A tall, shapely blonde with short curly hair stood next to him, leaning over to take a closer look at the strip. The blonde's scrubs, perfectly tailored to her curves, looked as if they had been spray-painted on her body. Santos bristled.

"Maybe we can run sometime?" the blonde asked. She flashed a dazzling smile at Patrick.

Stunned by a jolt of jealousy, Santos focused on the new woman with her perfect body and obvious attraction to Patrick. The rush of possessiveness and paranoia caught her off guard. Thoughts of the lovely Valentine's evening flew out of her head as she went on high alert to the competition.

Patrick turned around, saw her, and smiled warmly.

"Santos! This is Staci. It's her first day. She's been looking forward to meeting you." He sounded all business—naïve to the seduction underway.

Santos looked at Patrick, then Staci. She wanted to kill. Patrick seemed oblivious to what was going on—apparently he wasn't reading her emotions any more than he was aware of the blonde's flirtation. She watched as the potential rival stepped away from Patrick. *Does she sense my feelings?*

"Santos, I've been looking forward to meeting you. Heather has spoken so highly of you. I have so much to learn. I hope we'll become friends." Staci held out her hand to Santos. Her smile was genuine.

Santos struggled to respond politely. The uncontrollable jealousy that still swept through her required a fight for balance. She took a deep breath and reached out to shake Staci's hand. The hand that met hers was warm and firm. She managed to be gracious. "Welcome. Glad to meet you." She let out her breath. "Let me put away my things, and why don't we meet in the lounge and get started?"

"Sounds good to me." Staci stood up straight and smiled.

"Coffee later?" Patrick called out to Santos as she walked away. She nodded.

On her way to the lounge, Santos's thoughts went wild. *Oh God. She's tall, slim, and gorgeous. I'm short, petite,* and . . . pretty? I bet she has the metabolism of a sixteen-year-old boy. She's probably incredibly bright too. I don't run. She does . . . great!

BLAKE

The sun was setting on another long spring day. Kids chattered and giggled nearby, talking excitedly about the end of school, baseball, camp, and summer vacation. Spring in the south was in full bloom. The songs of migrating and mating birds filled the air. Wisteria bloomed wildly. Light rain showers knocked the pollen off the trees and ushered in crisp, clean air.

It was all lost on him.

His vampire-like need for flesh haunted him day and night. Every once in a while, when he keenly felt his isolation from the human race, he wondered why he was this way. He speculated it had begun as a child. A string of men who "dated" his mother had marked Blake's early years. One of them turned him on to porn, while another taught him a few things no six-year-old should know. Early on, he knew shame and embarrassment. He kept secrets. He had no friends.

Sex was his all-consuming need, and he didn't care much how he got it. Drugs made it easy. Drop the powder in the drink when his tasty morsel for the night headed to the bathroom, or mix it in a fresh drink from the bar. Even offer a pill to accentuate the high of alcohol. It was easy to hunt when a girl wanted to feel pretty and desirable, when she wanted to be with someone. Poor self-esteem kept him in business. Most women wanted to be with Blake. He had the formula for attraction down pat.

He had slept late during the day, showered and dressed for the night out. He usually moved from bar to bar to avoid discovery. Tonight he was staked out in a drinking hole popular with the college kids. He would make sure he picked up someone from out of town. There were always lots of girls looking for a guy. He reached in his jeans for the small bottle of pills and put one in the pocket of his shirt. That should be all it took. He was ready.

He took a swig of beer from his long-necked bottle of cold Shiner Bock. As he evaluated the meat market specialties of the night, he wondered when the pain of rejection had turned to rage. His early abandonment by his mother, who chose drinking and hooking up over mothering and love, had left him alone, cutting his heart. Over the years, scar tissue formed, and he separated himself more and more from the human race, allowing few to know him. He rarely opened his heart to anyone. *Who wants the pain?* He had made that mistake a couple of times—no more. The last one had been too recent. The one who burned him, the one who reeled him in like a fish on a hook, bewitched him with her body and her smile, and gave him hope that there might be something else, something more in life, had left him. *I thought she loved me.*

He shook off the thought and focused. The night was young. Let the fun begin. A young girl with long blonde hair was watching him from across the room. He smiled and nodded, took another sip of beer, and headed her direction.

He would find her yet.

Staci—she would pay.

SANTOS

The Pathways task force met for the first time at 6:00 a.m. The time worked well for both day and night shift members. With Emma and Heather out, Santos decided it was her turn to feed the crowd. She knew that food was a powerful reward, and staff rarely had time to eat. Maybe it was time to launch a monthly lunch or dinner during work potluck for the nurses, docs, pharmacists, and other team members? There was nothing like food to bond a family.

Last night she had started to put together a new breakfast casserole, chile unrellenos, from the cookbook *Chocolate for Breakfast*. With that name, any recipe in the book had to be good. The cookbook was from the grateful Gideon family, something they had found on their travels to Napa Valley. She finished assembling the dish before she left for work.

As the casserole baked in the small convection oven, the tantalizing smell carried the promise of hot food—luring staff to the lounge. Kamy had made her mother's pumpkin bread, and Kathleen brought fresh fruit, paper plates, and napkins. They arranged the food on the counter of the lounge.

Staci walked in carrying a box of warm kolaches from the nearby bakery.

"Trying to help out," she said with a smile.

She's too perfect, Santos thought, and immediately tried to banish the hostility from her thoughts. Her feelings about Staci had come a long way from her first impression; there was no need to lapse back into petty jealousy now.

Staci had been precepting with Santos for two weeks. She was an eager learner, a quick study, and open to feedback. She was also fearless—she jumped right in to try new things and was cool in a crisis, yet always knew when to ask for help. Santos had noticed gaps in Staci's knowledge, but she chalked that up to lack of experience in tertiary care. Staci asked for reading materials to study and opportunities to practice skills. She was always grateful for Santos's help. Contrary to her knee-jerk first impression, Santos was beginning to like the traveler, even respect her.

Nick and Patrick walked in, and Santos caught a hint of their conversation.

"Did you get it?" Patrick asked.

"Yep," Nick replied and smiled.

"Get what?" Santos asked, suddenly quite curious.

The room was noisy with conversation. Patrick didn't hear her.

"Nick, grab something to eat and let's get this started . . . next time, you're in charge of food," Santos called.

"I don't think you want me to do that," Nick replied.

"I'll help," Patrick replied. "We can do this, Nick." He smiled, piled a plate with food, and sat down.

"Been out for a run already?" Santos asked.

"Yes—it was a beautiful morning. I can tell spring is on the way!"

"Wasn't it gorgeous?" Staci replied. "The sky was clear and the stars so bright."

"They were," Patrick agreed.

Santos's heart sank. What was going on? Had they gone running together?

"Where do you usually run, Patrick?" Nick asked.

"I usually do the Rice University track or sometimes around Rice Village," Patrick replied.

"Saw you out there today," Richard replied. "I couldn't catch up with you."

Patrick laughed. "I'm still working off the calories from the chocolate sformato someone insisted I try on Valentine's Day." He looked at Santos and winked.

She smiled back but was still confused.

"Well, you were running like a bat out of hell when I saw you," Richard replied.

Santos shook off her obsession with who was running with whom and worked to keep her thoughts on the work at hand. "Time to get started, everyone. We have only so much time, and this is an important meeting."

"Yes, Boss," Nick replied.

Everyone found a seat, feasting on the sweet and savory food, and once one of the basics in Maslow's Hierarchy of Needs had been sated, they came to life with new energy.

Santos began. "Thank you, everyone, for taking the time to be here. We know you are all busy with life and work. But this may be some of the most important work of our careers. Dr. Whiting, would you like to kick this off with a few remarks?"

"Yes, thanks, Santos," Richard said. "Let's face the facts—people in our country have a tendency to deny death. They believe that health care can cure every patient. Because of this, many patients and families feel they have the right to extraordinary means to maintain life, even when there is no hope. Sometimes I think this is because they don't realize they have choices, and in other cases, they fear—death, the unknown, whatever—very likely because they have not prepared, emotionally or spiritually, for the fact that we all will die."

He paused to check his notes. "The rate of ICU use in

the last month of life has increased. In 2009, some 29.2 percent of people who died experienced an ICU stay in the last months of life. In fact, over 10 percent of people who died had three or more hospitalizations in the last three months of life. Hospitalizations are traumatic. They can expose vulnerable people to hospital-acquired infections, and they do not usually prolong life or decrease suffering . . . yet the American people continue to seek hospital care when hospice care would be more appropriate."

"There is fear of the term *hospice,* and most people don't understand the difference between palliative care and hospice. Just so we all start on the same page, palliative care can be given to a person of any age, at any time in life. It is not confined to any specific diagnosis. Palliative care's purpose is to reduce suffering by managing pain as well as other symptoms of disease, and increase comfort. Hospice, on the other hand, focuses on relieving symptoms and supporting patients and families with a life expectancy of months, not years. Palliative care is a part of hospice care. Hospice is about guiding a patient toward a peaceful death. End-of-life care, wherever it is delivered—at home, in the hospital, in freestanding hospices or hospital hospice beds—should be sensitive to the unique needs of patients and attend to the physical, psychological, social, and spiritual concerns of the patient and family."

"It's time for a new era in health care, where patients, families, and health-care providers begin to partner and make informed decisions at a most important time in the life cycle. It is time for us to start a new crucial conversation."

Richard put his notes down, leaned his elbows on his knees, and clasped his hands together, tucking them under his chin in a thoughtful pose. "It reminds me of another era, years ago, when our children were born. The natural childbirth movement, a partnership with families and health-care providers, changed the shape of obstetrical care. Fathers began to participate in cesarean births, hospitals built birthing centers, and we heard and adjusted to the needs of patients."

"Many years before this movement, when birth moved from the home to the hospital, we lost many mothers and babies. Bacteria were just being discovered, and the idea that you should wash your hands was foreign. Surgeons went from the autopsy suite to delivering babies without washing their hands. Later, new medications to control pain were experimentally tried on women in labor. There was no research, no FDA, no protocols. Pain medications were administered by mouth, by injection, by gas, and even by suppository. Mothers died of respiratory arrest from over-doses—the iatrogenic causes of death—things we did or did not do to mothers. But over the years health care advanced and research flourished. After years of discoveries, medicine advancing, it was time to take the best of both worlds and create the best and safest experience for childbirth."

"Today, we have a paradox at work. Health care and our professions have advanced tremendously, but the attitude of the American public has not necessarily changed about end of life. We have a big job to do—convincing our patients and families that they can have better quality of life by deliberately designing unique pathways to death. Yet, simultaneously, we will need to develop our systems to support their wishes."

Santos's heart remembered her experiences in both the beginning of life and death. "We know that every patient will have different preferences. In OB, we provided the moms and dads with checklists of choices for their experiences. When my mother was diagnosed with terminal colon cancer, it was already in her liver. She chose quality of life and turned down chemotherapy. When I asked her where she wanted to die, she looked me in the eye and said, 'I never want to go back to the hospital.' With the help of hospice, at home, we made that possible. She had six very good months, was up and active until the last month. She died in her own room. We were all with her, our dog was on her bed, candles were burning, and she died on her own terms, peacefully. It was beautiful."

"That is one Pathway, one choice," Nick said. "We need to create multiple pathways for our patients, teach them the choices they have, and then help them to find their way."

"This is going to be a challenge," Chaplain Smith added. "Every religion, every culture—as we've mentioned—has a set of beliefs. We need to be not only sensitive to these beliefs, but use them—"

Santos interrupted. "I'm thinking that the Pathway for each patient has multiple threads, or colors. Religion is one of them; culture another—"

"Their clinical situation," Nick added.

"Their family support," said Mary.

"Their legal wishes and how they've backed up their wishes with legal documents, like living wills," Melissa said. "The living will, also known as an advance directive, is probably one of the first places we should start. It's a way we can begin this conversation."

Richard jumped back in. "I know I'm repeating some of this, but we also have new members who have joined the group. We're approaching this in a very different way at this hospital. Instead of referrals to palliative care teams, we're trying to take a grassroots, comprehensive approach, with patients and families at the core—people who give informed consent. Then we wrap in the support they need based upon their wishes. Here at MCH, we're starting in CCU and hoping to create a template for a whole-hospital approach."

Into the excitement of the conversation, the door to the lounge opened. A petite woman wearing a crisp white lab coat, red blouse, and a black tweed pencil skirt with black high heels stepped into the room. Her posture was perfect, and her dark brown hair, cut in a short bob, framed her face. She wore a gold herringbone necklace and gold clips on her ears. She was carrying a small book.

The woman paused and looked around the room, not saying a word but looking as though she felt she had every right to be there.

"May we help you?" Santos asked. She struggled to remember if she had ever seen this impeccably dressed woman before. *Have to remember, if I want to look taller, high heels and stand up straight. Not sure I could do four-inch heels. Are they worth the sacrifice?*

Richard stood up. "Oh, I'm sorry, Sandra . . . I forgot you were coming to be introduced at this meeting, or I would have let the team know to expect you."

"That's all right, Dr. Whiting," she replied, smiling at him. Her voice was low, confident, and cultured.

"Folks, this is Sandra Bane, your new interim director," Richard said. "I hope you will give her your support." He looked around the room—heads nodded or looked down. No one looked at the newcomer. The room went quiet.

Santos felt anxiety paralyze the conversation. She struggled with her own concerns but spoke up to fill the silence. "Sandra, welcome—please grab a seat. We're in the middle of the meeting right now. Can we introduce everyone when we're finished? We're on a roll at the moment."

"Certainly," Sandra replied and found her way to a seat off to the side.

But the temperature in the room had cooled, and the dialogue stopped. Santos looked at the group and picked up that everyone was considering the impact the newcomer would have on their lives. The focus was moving from patient care to "How does this affect me?" Richard, who must have sensed that anxiety was replacing productivity, spoke up before Santos could figure out a way to jump-start the conversation again.

"Why don't we take a quick ten-minute break? Back at 6:40, everyone."

The room cleared with a stampede. Santos stayed, trying to be sensitive to the feelings and needs of the new manager. She approached Sandra with her hand extended.

"Hi, I'm Santos Rosa. Welcome to CCU."

"Santos." Sandra's comment felt perfunctory, and her handshake was quick and firm.

"I think everyone is a little anxious about having someone new. Heather hired most of the nurses . . . she's a great mentor and a wonderful nurse. Isn't she, Richard? Patrick?" Santos realized she was prattling, but her nerves made it hard to do anything else.

"It's okay. They'll come around—one way or another," Sandra replied with a knowing smile and a cool, direct stare that sliced right through Santos. Sandra looked through her as if she did not exist. The looked chilled her. She felt like an empty shell.

Heather? Emma? Where are you when we need you?

Patrick introduced himself, and Richard started explaining the process and team to Sandra. She was difficult to read. Santos excused herself and headed to the bathroom.

She walked in and immediately heard Kathleen say, "That's no Heather!"

"I think it's the Antichrist," Kamy replied from behind a stall door.

"Ladies, she could be right behind me!" Santos intervened. "Quiet down . . . give her a chance."

Kathleen shrugged and walked toward the door softly singing the opening lines from the Hall and Oates classic, "Maneater."

Kamy came out and checked to make sure the door to the restroom was closed. As she washed her hands, she said, "Her reputation precedes her. I've heard she's toxic and a climber. Manages up well, beats up those she doesn't like. Very smart, builds loyalty by rewarding losers who could never make it anywhere else. I think she just got divorced. Better keep your eyes on Patrick. Kathleen's right, she's a man-eater."

"Enough . . . enough! We need to give her a chance," Santos replied. "Besides, she's only here until Heather gets back."

"From what I understand," Kamy shot back on her way out, "she can do a lot of damage in a short time." The door closed behind her.

Santos stood in the silence of the restroom and sighed. A toilet flushed.

Oh great! Santos's heart sank. She was mortified.

The latch on the stall slid back with a click, and the door opened. Staci walked out, straightened her scrubs across her hips, and headed to the sink where she washed her hands carefully. She dried them, pulled lip gloss out of her pocket, and touched up her full lips. Smoothing a few unruly curls, she said to the mirror, "Il pesce puzza dalla testa."

"What does that mean?"

"It's an old Sicilian saying about leadership. It means, 'The fish rots from the head.' It means we're in trouble because Sandra, according to the intel you just heard, is bad news. She's our new manager. She's the head of the fish, and it sounds like she's poison in a lab coat. We're going to have to stick together."

Staci turned her back to the mirror and faced Santos. She placed both of her hands on Santos's shoulders, cocked her head to the side, and laser-locked her green eyes on Santos. "Girl, I've got your back."

Staci smiled and walked out of the restroom.

Santos was stunned speechless.

SANTOS

The next day, Santos sat in the lounge, eating yogurt and fruit from home while reading about end-of-life care. Focus kept eluding her. She tried hard not to think about Heather's breast cancer—every woman's fear—and what she would face in the treatment journey. Then there was Emma's absence and the turmoil the change in leadership was causing on the unit. She felt a terrible sense of loss that threatened to open the deep wounds that had just begun to heal. Then there was Patrick, school, orienting Staci—almost too much to absorb. She rubbed her temples, feeling a headache starting to build, and took a sip of jasmine tea. The tea soothed her.

Take one thing at a time. The only way she could successfully manage was to put on blinders, compartmentalize the swirling environment. Work was her salvation. It was her mission, her calling.

As she scanned the materials, she focused on the patients she had met over the past few months. Some were still in the unit, while others had transferred to other areas or facilities. She made a list of patients with their ages and diagnoses. She went through each name, jotted down notes, and asked the critical question: *Would I be surprised if this patient died within a year?*

Her heart sank when she realized that of the fifteen names on the list at least twelve would likely die in the next year. Four of the patients were on the unit right now: Mrs. Scalina, Mr. Hope-Simon, Mr. McIntire, and Mrs. Cartwright. The list of people with no living wills, Do Not

Resuscitate (DNR) orders, or Allow Natural Death (AND) plans was not complete. She knew that most patients who had suffered cardiac arrest in the unit would not survive to be discharged. If they did survive, they might be on a respirator and would likely have substantially reduced function. These days, with the increasing acuity of their patient population, it was rare to have a patient who survived fully functioning, like Mr. Gideon. Her patients were frail. She needed to tiptoe into the topic of end of life after discussing goals of care first with them and then with their families. She would ask Nick and Melissa to join her after she had broached the initial topic with each patient and found a degree of readiness. Though Melissa looked younger than her age, she was already a grandmother and had lived through the deaths of both parents. Her life experiences showed in her confidence and her ability to talk with all kinds of people from all walks of life.

No time like the present. It's not going to get any easier.

Santos rinsed out the empty yogurt container and tossed it in the recycling bin. She stacked her notes in a neat pile and tucked them into her locker. Then she washed the teacup and her hands and headed to Mrs. Cartwright's bedside.

Santos found Mrs. Cartwright dosing. She was a lovely, widowed Southern woman, who at seventy-three had three grown children and nine grandchildren. A picture of Mr. and Mrs. Cartwright, taken when they were much younger, rested on her bedside table. Mrs. Cartwright's long strawberry-blonde hair cascaded down her shoulders, blowing in the wind, and her husband was dark and handsome. They looked happy, smiling to the camera. The background was tropical. Hawaii?

Another of their "frequent flyers," Mrs. Cartwright

had suffered from congestive heart failure for years. Santos assessed her monitors, oxygen saturation, and cardiac rhythm. Her urinary output was much better, but only due to the diuretics that would move her fluids from tissue cells into the circulatory system and finally to the kidneys. She had been breathing easier than before, but her face, against her long faded hair, was pale. Her nose was red where the nasal cannula supplied additional oxygen. Santos made a mental note to treat the area with a dab of Vaseline.

"Hi, Honey," her patient said from the bed. Her deep blue eyes were sharp with wisdom. "Can you get me a sip of fresh water? My mouth is so dry."

"Absolutely," Santos replied. She filled the glass with fresh water. Mrs. Cartwright sipped gratefully. "Can I put some lip balm on your lips? It will help keep them from drying out. You've been doing a lot of mouth breathing when you sleep."

"Thanks, Santos . . . you're a dear." She sighed. "You have no idea how frustrating it is not to be able to do much of anything for myself. And it's so cold here!"

"Let me get your shawl. Germaine brought it in for you yesterday."

"That would be wonderful, thank you."

"I'd like to get you up in the recliner for a while. I'll change your sheets—get your bed fresh—and maybe we can talk about how you feel." Santos helped the fragile woman sit up and dangle her feet at the edge of the bed. She wrapped the multicolored, heavy wool shawl around her shoulders, put slippers on her feet, and guided her to the recliner.

Mrs. Cartwright dropped gratefully into the recliner, where Santos piled on more blankets and elevated her feet.

"That feels great . . . so good to get out of that bed. The

linens are making permanent creases on my skin." Mrs. Cartwright smiled, rubbed her legs, and covered up with the blankets. "You seem preoccupied today, Santos. Something you want to talk about?"

Santos turned around from making the bed and pulled up a chair to sit beside Mrs. Cartwright. "You don't miss a thing, do you?" She took her patient's cool hand in hers.

"Been around a long time, Dear . . . I'm pretty good at reading people. Just because I'm sick and old doesn't mean I've lost my brain. I have a lot of time on my hands these days with nothing to do but think." She smiled and patted Santos's hand.

Santos looked down at their hands and smiled. Then she looked into her patient's eyes and began to talk. She felt awkward at first, almost as if she might be violating Mrs. Cartwright's emotional space by bringing up such a personal topic. But she felt the obligation to protect and care for her patient—protect her from what could happen if she did not express her wishes. Clinical decisions would be made for her patient at a time when she should have choices about the rest of her life and how and where she would die.

"Mrs. Cartwright, I noticed that you don't have a living will on file."

Mrs. Cartwright frowned. "What's that?"

"A living will is a legal document that describes your wishes about the kind of medical care you want or don't want when you are no longer able to make decisions for yourself. Each state has a slightly different format, but the premise is the same—a living will and other supporting documents can . . . honor your wishes, taking the pathway you choose . . ." Santos stopped abruptly, uncertain where to go.

"To die? Is that what you mean?" Mrs. Cartwright smiled and squeezed Santos's hands. Her dark blue eyes pierced Santos's. "Honey, I've lived a long and good life. I'm tired. My hubby is gone, my children are married, and I'm at peace. I know there is another life for this tired old soul of mine. I've read every book about heaven that can be imagined." She smiled and took a few deep breaths. "I don't want to be in the hospital again . . . this ain't the Ritz, honey, as good as you are to me, and my body is failing. I'd rather be at home in my own house, in my own clothes, and some-day, when he's ready, I hope the Good Lord will welcome me to heaven."

Santos's heart surged with relief, and her eyes filled with tears at the woman's courage and conviction. Now it was her job to help get her where she wanted to be.

"I would like to ask a couple of colleagues to join us—to have a conversation, when you're ready—about what we're calling your 'Pathway.' You've already met Dr. Nicholas Landon, and I'd like to bring in Melissa Bentley. She's very knowledgeable about the legal aspects and can be a huge help to us. We can have this conversation whenever you're ready."

Mrs. Cartwright laughed. "Honey, I'm not getting any younger . . . or much better . . . but I do better in the mornings. Let's set it up soon. I'm ready."

SANDRA

Sandra reviewed her notes from the meetings with staff as she waited for Staci in her office. The one-on-one meetings were a treasure trove of information. While Richard had given her a brief overview, this was perfect—allowed her to fish for more.

She found that most people really wanted to trust, but she was new and therefore, a threat. It was a challenge to vary her style to entice them to talk. Becoming the friend, not the enemy, by smiling and finding personal issues in common, she was able to get them to share. She didn't care—whatever tactic worked, whatever achieved results. She wore many masks and could play the part of friend, co-conspirator, mentor, potential lover, superb clinician, confident manager. You name it; she could morph into it. It just depended on what guise was required to achieve success with the unit, create job security, and put another notch in her belt in the climb up the corporate ladder.

By appearing tearful and pretending to reminisce about days as a new graduate, she was able to entice young and vulnerable Kathleen to share her lack of confidence and fear of feedback. Kathleen longed for a mother figure to replace Heather. Sandra could play that part. Sandra concocted a story about a failed love affair with a surgeon and was able to tease out of Santos her conflicted feelings about Patrick. Making yourself vulnerable had its price and its prizes. Santos shared with Sandra her concern about balancing work and a relationship.

Kamy—she was a pistol, literally and figuratively;

probably not a good one to cross. She wasn't afraid of much. Patrick was reserved and professional—completely to the point in his responses. He didn't volunteer any juicy tidbits. He had obviously learned from his late father, the prosecuting attorney. *Keep to the point. Only say the absolute minimum to answer the question.* Perhaps a little flirtation with him would set Santos off? She'd find a way to get to him and Santos. It was important that she do so—in Emma and Heather's absence, staff seemed to rally around them. Patrick and Santos were gaining power as they became the unofficial leaders.

Richard was just grateful, relieved to have Sandra taking care of daily operations. She had him wrapped around her little finger. A sweet smile here and there delivered with results went a long way in managing up. Higher-ups—especially docs—loved it when they did not have to worry about the daily details. They could focus on their passions—patients, teaching, and research. Most of them disliked the technicalities and politics of management.

The one common thread through all the interviews was how much the unit missed Heather and how important the Pathways task force work was to them. They wanted to surprise and please Heather with their successes. They were so naïve.

She waited impatiently for Staci. She was late. Sandra disliked travelers and tardiness. Travelers were expensive—they could cost a hospital millions not only in fees but, in her experience, in medical malpractice claims.

"Sorry I'm late," Staci said apologetically when she appeared in the doorway of Sandra's office. "I had to finish up a couple of things with my patients, then hand them off to Santos. This won't take too long, will it? I'm a little worried about Mr. Haddington."

"Come in, sit down." Sandra smiled and welcomed her warmly. "Rest your feet. You must be tired. I'm sure Santos will keep a good eye on him. This won't take long."

"Yes. It's busy out there today. I haven't had a break since I arrived."

"Would you like a granola bar?" Sandra opened her desk drawer and offered one.

"No thanks, I'm good," Staci said.

"So, tell me a little about yourself." Sandra watched Staci sit up straighter, definitely on guard. She got the feeling Staci wasn't going to be an easy win. Sandra smiled and tried her break-the-ice line: "What would someone who knows you really well say about you?"

Staci looked visibly anxious. She played with her fingernails and looked down, annoying Sandra.

Sandra circled around, trying another question designed to bait. "What do you like to do when you're not working?"

Staci took in a deep breath. "I run, meet with friends for drinks . . . study a lot. This is all really new to me. I need to read about all the drugs, interactions, study about my patients."

Sandra's voice took on a sympathetic pitch. "Sounds like it's a bit of a stretch for you?"

"Well, I spent time working as an EMT before I was a nurse . . . but this is my first time in tertiary care. It's fast and furious and constantly changing. I don't want to hurt anyone."

Sandra smelled blood. "Have you had any close calls?"

"No, no—I'm just cautious. Santos has been wonderful—and Patrick. I just ask a lot of questions."

Sandra's thoughts darkened. *Damn them.* But she kept her face neutral and her tone friendly. There was something here. She zeroed in on her target, hunting for more.

"Do you have family in the area? What brought you to Houston?"

"I had a boyfriend—we broke up—who lived here. I followed him and really liked it. The Texas Medical Center is incredible."

"So no boyfriend now?"

"No."

Let's be girlfriends and talk about boys. "What do you think about Patrick?"

"You mean his clinical skills?" Staci didn't seem to get it. She'd try again.

"No, he's cute. Don't you think? And smart," Sandra said in a friendly way. "Quite a catch."

"He's in love with Santos," Staci blurted out.

"Oh? Guess I heard a little bit about that. How long have they been together?"

"I really don't know," Staci said in an end-of-subject tone.

Sandra was getting nowhere. *Time to probe a bit deeper.* "What about family? Where are you from originally?"

Staci hesitated, just enough for Sandra to wonder. What was it about this girl? She was hiding something—maybe a lot of things.

"I'm originally from the Midwest. A small town in Iowa."

"Oh, where? I know Iowa pretty well."

"I'm sure you've never heard of it—Mars."

Sandra shook her head. "Nope, never knew anyone from Mars." They both shared a conspiratorial laugh. She saw Staci visibly relax, but Sandra didn't follow suit. As relaxed and friendly as she was on the outside, Sandra was always calculating on the inside. Staci had her interest piqued. *Got to check her out a little more.*

"Staci, do you have a resume you can give me? I don't see one in Heather's files."

Staci bit her lower lip and nodded. "Sure. It needs updating. But I'll get it to you."

"Fine, that's great. Anything else you'd like to tell me?"

"Everyone's been great—super people—the best. As I said, I'm studying a lot trying to keep up, but so far so good."

"Fine. Well, my door is always open. If you have any issues or concerns—about anything—just let me know. I'm here for you."

"Thanks, I will. Everything's okay, really. I've got to get back. I'm sorry."

We're done here. Sandra turned to dial her phone, signaling the meeting was over. Staci got up and left.

Need to do a little research. What is she hiding?

STACI

"There is no greater agony than bearing an
untold story inside you."
Maya Angelou

The quiet, softly lit pub smelled like peaty single-malt
scotch and rosemary-laced shepherd's pie. Staci inhaled
deeply, relaxing, enjoying the moment. She had studied the
history of the pub, how the owners had collected treasures
from their travels all over the world. Architectural drawings,
oil paintings, and ancient swords that looked as if they had
once belonged to the French musketeers hung on the re-
claimed stone walls. Leather sofas and comfortable chairs
were clustered around huge distressed-wood coffee tables.
Burnished-brass hurricane lamps cast soft circles of light.
Couples were quietly talking, sipping drinks, sharing small
plates of food and paper cones piled high with crispy
pomme frites.

Staci had finally convinced Santos to have a drink with
her after work. The cozy pub on Montrose was just the
place for a quiet conversation and a light dinner in front of
the fireplace. Tonight, it was unseasonably cool for spring,
and the fire crackled, burning brightly while an occasional
errant spark would fly across the room. While Staci waited
for Santos to arrive, she considered her interview with Sandra. The interim director was one calculated woman. Her
evil was palpable. Staci could sense conflict brewing, but
she hoped Sandra would find another target. Yet she hated
to see the young nurses fall prey. People like Sandra moved

from person to person, zeroing in on the next victim, until they became a casualty of the war. She'd seen this happen in gangs. She would give Sandra lots of room and avoid her as much as possible. She would eventually have to create some kind of resume, but she'd stall her off.

Staci's phone vibrated and buzzed. She looked at it, puzzled. *Who has this number?* She answered quietly. It was Sam—a girlfriend from her past; the life she had left behind.

"Hi Sam, what gives? How did you get this number?" Staci asked, confused.

"I don't know—maybe you gave it to me and forgot," Sam offered. "How've you been?"

"Really good, got a new job—working in Houston in the TMC." Staci spilled her happy news before her brain registered the risk. *Damn!* Sam was always loaded with the juiciest tidbits of information, from who was sleeping with whom to where you could get the cheapest drugs. Staci's new life depended on putting time and distance between her two worlds. But maybe she was becoming too paranoid. She really had no one to talk to, and Sam was a great listener. They shared a history of tough times.

"Hey, I can't talk now. Can I call you later?"

"Yeah, let's catch up," Sam said.

Staci's internal alarm throbbed with the discomfort of angst. Yet she was torn. What would it hurt? It would be nice just to talk, so long as she didn't become one of indiscreet Sam's profiles. Sam's social media posts were prolific. Staci didn't want to be "tagged" and "shared" with the thousands of "friends" Sam had collected over the years.

Ruefully, Staci decided not to call back. Her gut signaled danger, and she'd already potentially blown it by mentioning her job. Hopefully not. She tucked the cell in her purse. She saw Santos looking for her at the entrance to the pub and waved to get her attention.

"So this is how the other half lives." Santos smiled and slid into the booth seat opposite Staci. She looked around the pub at people immersed in their food and intimate conversations. "This is great—lovely." She sighed. "Work has consumed my life. Moments like this make me realize it. I really don't know how to have much fun outside of work. It's school then work and the commute is really all I know. Patrick keeps trying to tell me."

"Santos, you're always talking to me about being present with my patients—being in the moment, listening, sensing, and feeling—not just focusing on the tasks. Maybe you need to be more present in your personal life? Ever heard of balance?"

"I think balance is a myth. I don't know if you can have it all. Something always seems to take priority." Santos thought for a moment. "Maybe that's what it's all about—priorities, mindfully setting priorities. Obviously, mine has been work. Pretty boring, don't you think?" Staci waited patiently for Santos to ruminate, enjoying the conversation. Santos had a way of going straight for the deeper things in life, and she enjoyed it.

"If you think about this room," Santos continued, "someone decorated it—wanted it to create a feeling, an ambiance—but they had an idea of what they wanted, a plan. It's almost as if we need to create a—I don't know if this is the correct word—but a lifescape of what we want our lives to be, deliberately. And most of the time, we go rushing from here to there, and the days blur by. I need to work on that. I need to pull out that Jon Kabat-Zinn book Carol gave me a few years ago. "

"Who was Carol?" Staci asked.

Santos looked around the room, and Staci wondered why Santos hesitated.

"Carol was a dear friend of my mother's. She took me under her wing when Mother died." Her eyes shone with tears, and she looked down at her hands. "She died suddenly last year."

"I'm sorry," Staci said and grasped Santos's hand. Staci was no stranger to loss. "Do you want to talk about it?"

"Not now . . . I'd just as soon talk about the present right now. There's too much about the past that is painful. And recently a lot of it has been coming to the surface."

"Okay, I understand," Staci said. "Tell me about the book." She tilted her head until she caught Santos's gaze and smiled to encourage her. Her heart had connected to Santos's pain. Santos smiled back. It felt so right, so peaceful, to have a conversation with someone who was obviously successful yet had experienced the trials of life.

"Well, he writes about mindfulness—about being in the moment, noticing. It's more than enjoying the moment. It is, as he says, almost about watching your thinking—and what you're thinking. It's very Zen. It's also about how the world we create is in our head—how we react to things determines our world. Maybe if I read a few paragraphs a day, it might help me get back on track."

"Sounds like a good idea. Can I borrow the book sometime?"

"Sure, I'll give you a copy. I have an extra."

"Thanks." Staci smiled and her heart filled with the hope of a solid friendship. Trying to steer Santos out of what appeared to be an emotional slump, she changed subjects.

"How's Patrick? What have you two been up to recently? Anything fun?"

Santos's smiled faded. "It's going to be a little difficult to find time with Patrick. As you've noticed, Sandra has split our schedules. She believes you need to learn from other mentors besides me. You're going to see more of him that I do."

"That Sandra—she's a bitch. Sorry, I try to save that word for special occasions. When I met with her, she probed me about you and Patrick."

"You didn't say anything, did you?" Santos looked alarmed.

"Nothing . . . nothing really. She was after information." Staci considered her blunder with Sandra and realized that Sam and Sandra were on parallel tracks—both used information as power.

"I already blew it when I blurted out to her that we were in love." Santos shook her head. "That was really stupid on my part. That's probably why she separated us."

Santos's comment made Staci angry. Though Santos was her senior, Staci felt so much older, wiser in the ways of the world.

"Well, we can do something about that . . . I can always switch with you. We can do it after she posts the schedules. Maybe she won't notice."

"Don't count on it. Besides, we'd need to find you another preceptor. With Emma gone, we're lean in experienced nurses. Sandra knows she's tied our hands for a while." Santos shook her head. "I should never have opened my mouth. We're professional about our relationship at work, always. And she wanted to hear all about it. It's my fault. I'm the eternal optimist about people—always hopeful. Sometimes it bites me."

"I know her kind," Staci replied. "Information is

power. She'll withhold it or use it as ammunition. She'll self-destruct someday . . . hang herself."

"How about we change the subject?" Santos responded seriously. She shifted gears and smiled warmly.

Staci nodded. "Got it."

Staci looked around the room and felt safe, for the first time in a long time. "You know, it wasn't until recently that I even knew a world like this existed."

"What do you mean? I'm realizing that I know very little about you."

Staci looked down at her beer. *What can I tell her?* She decided to trust her gut. Santos could be trusted. She felt at ease with her, and the conversation in the quiet pub felt like a sanctuary. She could not remember the last time she'd been in a situation with another person where she could let down her guard without fear.

"I grew up in foster homes. Never knew my parents, was shuttled from here to there. I don't have a family or history to share. No memories of happy times around the Christmas tree. Thanksgiving was sometimes spent in a shelter. I have a story, but I don't really have any traditions—there is no family attic to search for treasures, no blood relatives, no photo albums." She quietly laughed, letting her mind go back to some of the happier memories. "I did have some happy times, especially when I was taken in by a black Baptist family. We got all dressed up when we went to church, hats and everything. I realized I could sing. We sang in the choir. It made prayer fun . . . inspirational. They were lovely, good people, but it didn't last. The dad died of a heart attack. It was really sudden—he was middle-aged—and they couldn't keep me any longer."

Staci stopped and looked at Santos. She saw compassion, but not pity.

"Go on," Santos said.

"On the streets, I was all about seizing the moment—the no-consequences model. I was fearless and faceless, moved on when I got tired of things or they went sour. I got a gun . . . learned how to shoot." Staci watched Santos lean back in her chair.

"Then I fell in love—with the wrong guy. Chemistry is not a compass that can guide you to the right man. I think you know that. It's not love. It can be a killer. Think about every character flaw and evil twist a man can have, and that was Blake. He was dangerous. I panicked. So I ran. I had to put a lot of territory between him and me." Staci stopped to gauge Santos's reaction. *So far so good.* "I realized I had to be able to take care of myself . . . no one was going to take care of me."

Santos's brow creased with worry, but Staci had to go with the flow. Time to tell the story even she wanted to believe. She blurted the words quickly. "So I got my GED, went back to school, became a nurse. I took the long way—the bumpy path. But I've got great instincts, a solid work ethic, and for the first time in my life, I've found a purpose in the CCU—with you and the rest of the team."

Santos said nothing but reached across the table and warmly squeezed her hand. Staci felt vulnerable, but she wanted to say more. She leaned forward and whispered, "I feel as if I've just been born."

To her surprise, she was struggling not to cry. A lump was building in her throat. She felt free and hopeful for the first time in her life.

Santos nodded, and her eyes were warm with understanding. Staci choked out, "And—most importantly—I think I found a friend."

Santos smiled and said, "You have a friend."

Relief flooded Staci. The tip of her story was out now. The iceberg of her past, and all that lurked below, could stay there.

"I can give you a family too," Santos said, smiling. "You may regret it—but I'd love to have you come share one of our family meals with us. If you can handle it." She laughed.

"I'd love to!" Staci felt happier than she'd ever remembered, but her instincts were kicking in, and she knew it was time to change the subject, shift the conversation away from herself.

"Enough about me." Staci took a sip of her beer and leaned back. "Tell me about it . . . how is it?"

Santos looked confused. "How is what?"

"The sex, girl, the sex . . . the chemistry between you and Patrick is like waves of Southern summer heat. It shimmers around you."

Santos pushed back her chair, and her eyes went wide. Staci felt a burst of shock as she translated Santos's reaction. She reached across the table, grabbed Santos by the forearm, leaned in and whispered, "You haven't done it yet?" Was Santos gay? No—she would have picked that up. "You're not a virgin, are you?"

"No, no." Santos sighed and shook her head. "But it's been so long, I might as well be."

Staci could not believe she was having this conversation. For the first time in a while, she didn't feel prepared to respond to what she was hearing. "Whew, that's a relief." She made a play at wiping sweat off her brow. "I haven't had to coach a virgin—ever. Don't think I've ever *known* a virgin."

Santos laughed. "Oh, Staci . . . enough!"

"Got protection?"

"Not yet."

"What are you waiting for? When the time is right, you want to be ready. Don't be stupid."

"You're right . . . I need to see my doctor, get a prescription."

"I had a foster mother who used to say, 'No matter how old a woman is, she has to be prepared for sex. All men have to do is lock and load.'"

"Okay, Staci . . . enough. I get the message." Santos blushed.

Staci leaned forward, back in control of the conversation. "I'm serious, girl. He wants to take it to the next level." She paused. "You love him, don't you? The way you look at him . . . your eyes shot flames of jealousy when you met me. You've got to love him."

"I love him—as a friend. We have a short but long story. Sometime I'll tell you about it." Santos stopped to sip her drink. "But I don't know if I'm ready to commit—if I have the time or the energy."

"We were just talking about missing moments—and being in the moment—and here you have a man who obviously adores you. Whoever knows if it's the right time? You'll never know if you don't try. Believe me, I've done enough bad experimenting and taking plenty of risks and made awful mistakes, but this is not risky. Yes, you risk your heart. But I can't think of a safer bet than Patrick."

Staci smiled and paused to look into Santos's eyes. She saw hope.

"We've got to trust that everything is in our lives for a purpose, the good and the bad, the sad and happy . . . learn from it . . . embrace it. Enjoy the happy times because they're like bubbles—they're fragile. They break."

She had Santos's attention, and Santos sat back and

spoke. "I know that, but I don't always embrace life the way I should. I've felt like a ping-pong ball recently, bounced around by deaths, being a victim . . . I don't want to even think back to the last year. I need to start making happy memories."

Something very serious must have happened last year. Staci wondered what. Since Santos obviously was not ready to talk about it, she would ask later.

"Santos, I'm in your life for a reason. You're in mine for a reason. You give me hope—that there is another way, another life. You and Patrick, your love is so fresh and new. It's . . ." Staci's eyes filled with tears, and her throat choked with emotion, ". . . so beautiful that it makes me happy just to watch you two. The little glances you give each other when you think no one is looking, the way he looks at you—like you're the only woman in the world."

Staci stopped to wipe a tear from her eye. She was flooded with a sense of vulnerability that surprised and frightened her. Her first glimpse of true love gave her hope. She reached across the table to squeeze Santos's hand. "Don't lose this gift by trying to stay in control. Life doesn't work that way. Trust me, if anyone should know that, it's me. Just when we think we've got control—we lose it."

SANTOS

The next morning, Santos hurried in to the conference room and took the last seat in multidisciplinary rounds. She glanced over at Sandra. The woman's long, perfectly red lacquered index finger tapped her wristwatch in warning. Santos's anger flashed, but she caught herself from spearing Sandra with her eyes. She looked away.

Sandra turned and smiled at Richard. "Would you like to begin?"

Richard smiled back, charmed.

Santos's heart sank. Would he ever see through this woman? Santos had been hopeful about Sandra at first, giving her a chance. But every day, she learned more and more about the so-called "leader" that made her angry and concerned. She wondered how someone like Sandra made her way into management. Bullies were dangerous among the staff, but lethal as leaders.

The one-on-one meetings with staff were over, and Santos found herself the unwilling recipient of their woes. Kathleen had shared her sensitivity about feedback with Sandra. Sandra immediately set up routine meetings, collected anonymous peer review reports, and shared them, unedited, word for word, with Kathleen. The feedback, while important, was harsh and delivered without compassion. It was killing Kathleen's sweet spirit. Kathleen was still recovering from the year before, and Santos regularly found her crying on the stairwell or in the bathroom. And she wasn't the only one who Sandra was abusing.

Santos did not know who she could talk to about

Sandra. With all her heart, she wanted to be supportive and honor Richard's decision to appoint her. But she was worried. Sandra was toxic. The situation was dangerous, not only for staff, but for the patients. Stressed-out, unhappy staff evolves into disengaged staff—a recipe for poor patient care, mistakes, and low patient satisfaction.

Melissa Bentley caught her eye and smiled from across the room. Always the professional, Melissa was dressed in a lavender business suit, her shoulder-length blonde hair in a tasteful flip. Santos acknowledged her with a nod.

Maybe I could talk to Melissa? She's smart and has been around the block. Could help me put everything in perspective. Make sure I'm not overreacting.

"Not only do we have patients to review today, but we have a number of other items to discuss," Richard began. "So if I could have everyone's attention. Santos, do you and Nick want to give us a Pathways update?"

"Happy to," Santos replied. "Nick, I'll start and then you jump in . . . okay?"

"Got it."

"The way we see this process is sort of like a DNA strand, with multiple components. We look at the patient's clinical picture and determine if he or she is a candidate. Then we wrap that with the patient's legally expressed wishes about end of life. Then we add in the other strands of everything from religious views to limitations at home. It's pretty complicated, but we have a preliminary list of candidates we'd like to run by this group. Our next step would be to get their attending doc involved and set up a crucial conversation with the patient." Santos looked around the room to assess understanding. It looked like everyone was tracking with her. "Nick will begin with the clinical case, and then Melissa will follow with the legal point of view."

Nick began. "Today, we probably have at least 25 percent of our patient population who are terminal. In tertiary care, we're going to see a higher percentage of patients who are here because this is their last resort. Fifty percent of them are over sixty-five. We're going to focus on those, since younger people will have other compounding issues, and we need to start slowly. Some of these patients are hoping for a surgical miracle, like a transplant or valve replacement—others for medical management. They are all in various stages of cardiac disease, and they will die likely within the year. What we don't want to do is have them fail and then do CPR or start life support on them when we know they are not going to make it."

Nick paused, and Santos stepped back in. "The American Association of Critical Care Nurses actually has a partnership initiative that has been underway for several years with the ABIM Foundation. It's called 'Choosing Wisely.' The focus is on helping health-care practitioners and patients to partner in making decisions. One of their many recommendations is that life support not be continued without offering the patient and family choices that may include comfort only. It's always easier to have this conversation before the patient clinically crashes. Our goal is to get ahead of the clinical course of disease and be prepared to honor patient wishes."

Sandra stepped in. "Did anyone see that article in the *Wall Street Journal?* Fundamentally, it was about getting patients more actively involved with their health care. The lead was particularly compelling, calling patient involvement 'the last mile in the race to fix health care.' It's quite good. The article talks about the high percentage of 'unengaged' patients who take a passive role in managing their health and health care. I would suggest you all access it online."

Melissa chimed in, "I have more information to support that opinion, Sandra. Less than 5 percent of our target patient population has living wills. That is very sad and could derail this whole process. To me, it's a signal that they haven't thought much about the end of life . . . and they may not have had any conversations with their family."

"I know we have patients and families who are ready to be on a Pathway, but we also have many patients who are not ready—and may be very resistant," Patrick offered. "For one, the McIntire family is a real challenge. Mr. McIntire is in end-stage cardiac failure, diabetic, nearing the need for dialysis. At nearly ninety, they want everything possible done—even experimental therapies. He's very close to total system shutdown, and they can't seem to let go. I'm at a loss as to how to help them find peace with dying."

"I find that patients and families that have drifted away from their spiritual roots—whatever they might be— have a harder time with life's challenges. And death is the ultimate challenge," Chaplain Smith added.

"And I hate to say this," Patrick added, "but their needs take me away from patients who *are* going to make it. We aren't an ER with triage here. We offer everyone the same level of care."

"Patrick," Sandra spoke up, "what are you going to do about that? To be an effective nurse and leader, you must have some influence with the family—get them on the right track."

Patrick let her comment go unanswered. Santos rushed in to redirect the conversation before it made Patrick a target. "Family and their unresolved issues or concerns can really complicate decisions, especially if they're not on the same page. I'm thinking of Casey Kasem. Didn't a judge have to intervene to withhold food and fluids from him to allow him to die? Wasn't that because the family disagreed about how his last wishes should be honored?"

"Yes. That's correct," Melissa responded. "If you look at them in total, many of our ethics consults are around physicians and families that disagree on a course of action. That said, we believe that we could get living wills up to 25 percent. The number should be much, much higher for the unit. But this is going to have to start with each patient's physician, in the doctor's office."

"That's a good long-term plan," Sandra said. "But we have issues in the here and now. Every patient who is a hopeless cause is a drain on the system."

The room was silent as the callousness and chill of her statement sunk in.

Mary Collins chimed in. "Every patient who enters a hospital should have a living will, but as we've discussed, denial is a very powerful coping mechanism, and many people do not know they have choices when they're in the hospital. It's our obligation to advise them of their choices. It is their *right* to choose. When they choose, we can help support them."

"So," Santos picked up the thread of the conversation from Mary, ignoring Sandra's point of view, "if we work from at first two directions—is the patient a clinical candidate and does he or she have a living will that truly expresses their current wishes—we have a preliminary list of patients. In reviewing the literature—and I want to remind everyone that all of this information is on our unit intranet site under the Pathways Task Force heading—we are going to pilot this using guidelines for the crucial conversation. I found the template in a CME course developed by Dr. Laurie Barclay. The template we're recommending was published in the *Canadian Medial Association Journal.* The format for the conversation is called SPIKES. I'm going to pass around a sheet for you to take a look at while we talk."

"Santos, have you involved any patients or family members in the task force yet?" Sandra asked.

"We are just about ready. We need to get this going, but we realize that these dialogues can very sensitive. I did test the waters with Mrs. Cartwright. The moment was right, and she was very receptive to having a conversation about her end-of-life wishes."

"Well, at least that's *something*," Sandra responded sharply.

Nick rallied. "We want to test-drive the SPIKES format with some patients who may not qualify, just to get their input, and definitely include family members in the conversation."

"SPIKES is an acronym for Setting up, Perception, Invitation, Knowledge, Emotions, Strategy, and Summary," Santos continued. "You can see from the handout that we first need to set the stage for the interview so that the patient feels safe and trusts the person or persons conducting the interview."

"I think it might be best to plant a seed with a patient and family first before setting up the full-blown interview," Richard added.

"We agree," Nick replied, and all members of the task force nodded.

"That's what I did with Mrs. Cartwright," Santos added.

Melissa spoke up. "Since the interview covers not only their perception and knowledge of the medical situation but also how they feel, we believe this should be a multidisciplinary discussion—probably no more than two people at a time, though, so as not to overwhelm the patient."

"I would suggest some dry-run role plays with clinicians . . . wouldn't you, Richard?" Sandra asked.

"Excellent idea, Sandra—practice on each other first and give one another feedback." He looked around the group. "Isn't she a great addition to our team?"

Santos managed a small smile and watched as many of the people in the room avoided eye contact with Richard. No one said a word.

Sandra ignored the lack of response. "Even though I would suggest role-playing, we really need to get this program going. I promised Elaine we would have some good results by the end of the month. Seems you are all focusing a great deal on process. We need to move that to results."

Santos, annoyed with Sandra's lack of compassion and understanding, felt her defenses go up, not only for herself but for her team. Sandra made it sound like they'd been wasting time, but the process was essential for the work to be successful. "We're all learning about this. It's all new, and we need to study and practice. That takes a little time."

Nick nodded. "Most clinicians don't know how to have these kinds of conversations with patients and families. It's a delicate subject and very important. I don't think I even know the words to say to begin the conversation. We've been so focused on *cure* that we sometimes totally miss the patient's point of view. We push our practice, our personal need to save them, on the patients. For some of us, this is a total shift in practice."

"I'm really new at this," Staci added. "I don't even know if I can find the words to have these conversations."

"Me too," Kathleen added. "It's hard enough for those of us who have never faced dying in our families to have these conversations. I can't imagine talking about this with my grandmother."

"We hear you," Richard said. "We need time to practice in order to achieve sound results. It's okay to make a mistake now and then."

"I'm really uncomfortable making a mistake in this area," Nick said.

"Well, maybe you aren't the right the person to co-lead this team." Sandra's eyebrow arched as she glared at Nick.

The room went quiet as tension crept up another notch, stretching already taut nerves and raising the temperature in the room. The conflict was obvious.

"I'm not a quitter." Nick's eyes flashed dark with anger. "Santos and I, with the rest of the team, will do the best job we can."

"You know, folks, this isn't a hotel or a spa. It's a hospital. It's a business," Sandra said.

Santos watched as Richard did a quick turn and flashed a quizzical look at Sandra. Sandra, glaring at Nick, missed Richard's look.

Santos was proud of Nick for pushing back and glad Sandra was starting to show her true colors in front of Richard, but she couldn't let this continue to derail the meeting. She decided to try to diffuse the conflict by playing Sandra's game by her rules. She knew Sandra's agenda—results and fast. She did not care how they got the work done, just get it done.

"We hear you, Sandra. We'll accelerate our work, and I'll give you a report by the end of this week with the names of the patients we've tentatively identified." She hoped that would give them some breathing room.

"That sounds good, Santos," Richard replied. "Let's

all talk about it at the end of the week."

Rounds continued without further comment. The clinicians and their multidisciplinary partners got up to leave the room.

"Oh, before everyone heads out, we need to plan our next meeting," Santos said. "Nick, you had an idea you wanted to share?"

"Yes, briefly—I've been hearing about music therapy and its impact on patient relaxation and healing—not necessarily physical healing, though it can help that, but emotional and spiritual well-being. As we explore the therapies that ease a patient from this life and increase the comfort of passing, it's important that we look at the research and practices that include one of life's most potent healers—music."

Mary jumped in. "It's wonderful! It's being used in many hospice and palliative care settings. Can I help with the next meeting? There's a lot of research out there and some good programs."

"Mary, sounds great!" Santos replied.

"We also have a lot of clinicians who are musicians," Nick added. "We know how it makes us feel—the euphoria it brings—and how much we enjoy listening to music as well as playing it. There is research out there on how music interacts with the brain. There are professional organizations and journals that study the application of music in clinical practice. If we're going to reinvent how our patients die, we need to integrate music into patient care."

"Well, we've got a lot of work to do," Sandra cut in, her tone just south of icy. "And people—patients are waiting."

Sandra left the room abruptly, and the team got up to leave. Santos felt dismissed and shut down. She walked out with Nick. Melissa and Kamy were waiting for them in the hall.

"Bitch," Nick said under his breath. "I was hoping to make an announcement, but damn if I will with her in the room."

"Nick, we'll get it done . . . we're smart and fast workers. Try not to let your feelings show so much."

"She'll use them against you." Melissa said. The tall, blonde attorney from Louisiana raised a knowing eyebrow and stared directly at Nick.

Santos was surprised to hear Melissa speak up. The lawyer always watched what she said, most often saying nothing, always observing and analyzing the situation.

"I told you," Kamy said to Santos. "Anything she learns, she will use against you."

Santos sighed in frustration. She hated to gossip about a director, but Sandra's agenda was obvious to everyone by now, and it was starting to interfere with the real needs of the people in their care. "She has no idea of what this is going to take . . . of how change requires learning a new way of behaving, and that takes time. Some people are ready, others are not."

"Remember, she always wants to hear the truth," Kamy added. "That's because she has no empathy. She doesn't care about anyone but herself—about how she looks. If we make her look bad, we're dead. She's going for Heather's job. I'd bet anything on it."

"Okay, everyone, enough venting," Melissa stepped in. "Let's get back to work, show her what we're really made of. We don't want our patients to suffer."

Santos nodded, fighting to push back her own anger. Sandra was being totally unreasonable. She had no clue how complicated this work was and the pressure and conflict it generated. Her lack of insight was not going to make their jobs any easier. Helping patients and their families understand that there might be another way to die would be difficult. It was almost overwhelming to think about all the work they had to do to change not only clinical practice, but society. Sandra and her unrealistic demands were not going to make it easy. How could someone be a nurse and be so cold?

"Snap out of it, Santos," Nick said. "Isn't that what your mother used to say to you? Mine did . . . I want to change the subject to something good."

Santos smiled. "I'm all for it. What do you have in mind?"

"Anyone want to hear my announcement?" Nick smiled broadly and spread out his arms.

"Announcement?" Santos replied, wondering how he had recovered so quickly.

"So Nick, what do you have to tell us? Buy a new car?" Kamy asked.

"Something better than that." He looked around to see who was near. The coast was clear. He proudly announced, "I'm getting married. I asked Nancy last night."

Tears filled Santos's eyes, and she reached out to hug him. "Oh, Nick, I'm so happy for you! We thought from the beginning that you two were a match."

"Congratulations, Nick," Melissa said, smiling. "Tell us about the wedding—when and where."

"Well, since she's from South Dakota, we're going to have it there—when things warm up and before I start my fellowship in July. It's going to be a really small wedding, just family. They don't have a lot of money. So we thought we'd like to celebrate here in Houston with a party. What do ya'll think about that?"

"Sounds great!" Santos said. The others added their agreement.

"We thought since we work with a bunch of closet musicians that we might do a sort of 'no host' party at Mother's—you know that club? We can't reserve the whole club, but we can take over the stage and have some fun," Nick replied. "I want to surprise Nancy with the party— I'd love to pay for the whole thing, but we are starving residents—with Emma gone—me especially." Nick reached down to clutch his stomach, and he laughed. His scrubs hung on his lanky frame. "We're going to be paying off our medical school student loans till the day we die."

Santos put two and two together, remembering that Patrick had mentioned something about Nick and Nancy getting ready to take it to the next level. "Does Patrick know about this?" Santos asked suspiciously.

"Yeah, but I swore him to secrecy. Sorry Santos. He helped me pick out the ring. Can you imagine that picture? Two clueless guys, trying to look intelligent." He looked giddy with happiness. Thoughts of Nick and Patrick together in a jewelry store made Santos smile.

While Santos's mind considered the details of the party, her heart remembered Kimberly's wedding and those of her many college friends. The many bridal showers she had helped host, the weddings attended, and now baby showers were popping up here and there. Would her time ever come? She shook off the self-absorption and focused on Nick.

"Can we help you plan it? We really need to have some fun."

It was time to create a diversion. Time for the team to focus on a new nemesis. Spend a little more energy, run them in circles—break them.

She took a look at the Pathway list. There were some patients who should be on this list—wasting resources, they were never going to leave the unit alive. She had made it a point to visit all patients, so they were comfortable seeing her and would not be surprised if she came to their bedside. She had knowledge, opportunity, and access—a trifecta, the winning combination.

She had a virtual candy store of options to choose from: pumps, pills, pushes—then of course, missed doses, adjusting lab results, turning off cardiac monitor alarms. Then there was adding too many or little electrolytes, bumping up the morphine or lidocaine. Infections were always possible, but that might take too long. Air in the line was another option— that would be quick and easy, no trace.

They were going to die anyway. Did it really matter how and when?

The chaos it would create and the pain of their loss would disturb the team and amuse her. The game was clear. It was time to play.

BLAKE

He let the water run in the shower, thinking. Where was she? He *had* to find her. The little scores he had made along the way were not enough satisfy his craving or distract him from the hunt for the ultimate catch, the woman who was rightfully his. He needed more every time. His addiction was all consuming. And once the thrill of the conquest was over and the adrenaline spent, he fell into a black mood, depressed and angry, unsatisfied. It was getting worse. *How to find her?*

Social media might work. But he wasn't into that. He didn't want the history. His mind worked rapidly. Who would know where she was? She didn't have friends to speak of, though when they were a couple they'd hung out with Dylan and Sam. Now Sam, she was a social media junkie—probably slept with her phone. He'd lost track of her since Staci left him, and that was months ago. She was Staci's friend so he didn't have her number. But she was the key.

He had to find Sam. How? An idea popped into his head. *Brilliant!*

Blake finished showering, dressed in jeans and a T-shirt. He drove to a store that sold sports equipment and paraphernalia. He couldn't decide whether to buy a Longhorns or Aggie sweatshirt, and he finally decided on the burnt orange University of Texas. He paid for his purchase, put it on, and drove over to Denton where he might find a supply of young, computer-literate women from Texas Women's University. He found a coffee shop close to campus and parked.

Saturday afternoon, the coffee shop was full of young people plugged into their computers. Some were studying, books and papers piled high on the table, while others watched videos and small groups sat drinking coffee. He stood in line, bought a cup of coffee, and sat where he could watch.

Found one.

A young woman sat alone, head bent over the computer. Strings of long, light brown hair hid her face. Fixated on her computer screen, she absentmindedly twirled her hair around her fingers while she scanned Facebook. She was the kind of girl a guy on the prowl would miss. She blended into the woodwork. She was wearing baggy blue jeans, flip-flops, and a sweatshirt. He took his coffee and walked over. There was an empty chair at her table for two.

"Hi. I was wondering if you could help me."

She looked at him suspiciously. "I don't know—what do you want?"

"I'm trying to find a friend of mine. My phone crashed, and I lost all my contacts. I was wondering if I could find her on Facebook?"

"That's possible . . . you can sign in to your account and try to friend her."

"That's my problem. My computer was stolen, and I don't have a Facebook account." He smiled. "I was really stupid . . . left my laptop in the car. Someone broke in and stole it. I haven't put together enough cash to buy a new one yet." He smiled at her. His dark eyes looked deeply into her pale blue ones in his best attempt to look trustworthy. He watched her face change to one of sympathy. *Got her hooked.*

"Think you could you help me set up a Facebook account and see if she's out there? Buy you a cup of coffee?"

She paused and gave him a good look. He was the best-looking guy in the room. He knew it. She knew it.

"Why not?" she said.

"Thanks, you're a doll." He asked her how she liked her coffee and bought her a fresh cup. Then he pulled out the chair, straddled it, and pulled it close to her.

"You smell good," he said. "Like cookies." He smiled. "I'm sorry, I don't even know your name."

"It's Marci . . . and thanks, but I'm not sure how I *could* smell like cookies." He could tell she didn't believe him, but she liked his attention anyway.

"I'm Blake," he said and reached out to shake her hand. Her grip was cool and limp, just fingers to hold, not palm to palm. The weak grip told him a great deal that might be useful later.

"Let's get started," she said. "First, we need to set up a Facebook account for you." She guided him through all the steps and set up a password. "You can upload a picture later. Now, who do you want to find?"

"Her name is Sam Cotter."

"Okay, let's see what we can find." She typed in the name. A long list of pictures with names appeared. "Do you see her?" Marci looked at Blake. They were sitting nearly head to head looking at the computer screen.

Blake peered at the screen as she scrolled through the scores of names.

"That's her!"

"Sure?"

"Yep!"

"Okay, let's send her a friend request and see if she responds." Marci typed and talked. "You know, some people may take quite a while to respond."

"Well, I may just have to circle back with you," he said, smiling. "Until I get a computer." She smiled back and then looked at the screen again.

"Well, look at that!"

"What?"

"She friended and instant messaged you!"

"I figured she'd be connected 24/7," he said. "Can you ask her for her phone number?" Marci typed. "Got it!" she replied and read it to him. He wrote it down.

Done. Now on to a new mission.

"Darlin', thanks so much for your help. Maybe we can get together someday?" He leaned down to give her a chaste kiss on the cheek. She blushed.

He tucked the note in his pocket and walked out the door. *Marci, you're a lucky girl. Good thing I have bigger fish to fry.*

Time to speed things up. The Pathways Task Force was taking too much time. Study this and study that—once decisions were made they should be followed by action. Time to take things into her own hands. She hated depending on others to achieve results. It was much easier to just do it.

It didn't take more than a moment to figure out who would be first. She liked to do unannounced night rounds. She had a regular routine of round-the-clock visits. This time she was on a mission.

She slipped quietly into the unit while the night shift was finalizing their charting. She even spotted one of them asleep in a chair by a patient's bed. She made a mental note of that. She had collected her supplies before leaving the previous day, and the syringe was filled and ready to go.

She took a quick look down the hall and saw no one. She went to Mr. McIntire's bed and pulled the curtain closed. This would take ten seconds. He was sound asleep. She'd seen to that before she left last night—adding another dose of morphine. She took the syringe of potassium, inserted it into the IV port, and pushed slowly. Then she ran saline to dilute the push—to give her enough time to get away before his heart started to show ventricular fibrillation, the most likely lethal arrhythmia. It was too bad they would have to waste money on a code. But that couldn't be helped. She picked up the syringe and left as quietly as she came. The cafeteria and her morning coffee beckoned.

SANTOS

Santos dreaded meeting with Sandra, but she had promised her the list of Pathway patients and potentials. Even in a meeting with everyone else present, Sandra made her anxious and sucked her energy dry. Being in close quarters, one-on-one, was the worst possible situation.

She had prepared carefully for the meeting with an agenda, notes, and a few journal articles for Sandra to read. She steadied her nerves with deep breaths and put on her "yellow slicker," a mental model of protection designed to let things just slide off her. It was something her mother had suggested many years ago, and it worked.

She found Sandra in Heather's office. Sandra had carefully stripped the office of any sign of Heather. Gone were the fresh flowers in the blue glass vase, the crystal bowl of assorted candies and chocolate, and the family pictures of smiles on the beach and in the mountains. Heather always kept a slush fund of small bills in case someone needed money for lunch, the light rail, or a coffee. She was generous with her staff. Her office had always been a safe haven to share, to receive feedback, to work through issues, and to cry.

Sandra had taken ownership of the office like she had of everything else. She'd populated the office with her art and symbols—some minimalist prints in black frames and a few pieces of sculpture, cold like she was. No pictures to tell her personal story. Her diplomas were front and center, as were her awards. There were few papers on the desk, expressing Sandra's distaste for clutter. She primarily worked electronically, though when Santos stood in the doorway, she did see Sandra slip a file away in her briefcase and lock it.

"You wanted the list of patients?" Santos asked.

"Yes, thank you, Santos." Sandra smiled as if they were best friends. It didn't fool Santos for a moment. *I'm giving her what she wants. I'll be in her good graces for a day, maybe. Hopefully she'll target someone else for a while.* She quickly rebuked herself for wishing Sandra on someone else. The unit felt like it was under guerilla attack. Who would be next?

Santos sat down in a chair that was decidedly lower than Sandra's. *Another power tactic.* Taking a deep breath and making sure her yellow slicker was in place, Santos explained to Sandra how the patients had been selected. She gave her the materials to read and updated her on the progress of the task force. She called her attention to the fact that some were not on the unit, while others were.

Santos's mouth was dry. It took every ounce of her self-control to respectfully brief Sandra. She knew that Sandra was a hypocrite who cared little about the patients or families—or even the Pathway plan of care. Sandra was a great actress. "The Task Force has decided to focus on Mr. Hope-Simon, Mrs. Cartwright, and Mrs. Scalina. Mr. McIntire could have been another candidate, but as you heard in report, he died last night."

"Yes, too bad," Sandra responded with the same amount of concern she might express if the dress she wanted in her size was not available. She showed no hint of compassion. Santos kept her anger in check. *Just got to get through this meeting.*

Sandra quickly shifted gears back to the subject at hand. "You want to start with some quick wins first?"

"Yes, sort of—their wishes are in concert with the goals of Pathway and they're ready."

"Thank you, Santos. You *can* achieve results. I'll read your materials and catch up with you if I have any questions."

Sandra picked up the phone and began to dial—no good-bye, no more questions. The meeting was over. Santos got up and gratefully escaped to her patients.

SANTOS

"When words leave off, music begins."
Heinrich Heine

Santos and Patrick had agreed to meet at Dosey Doe for dinner and the concert. Since the restaurant was on the I-45 feeder, it would be an easy drive home for him. They both had to work the next day. As it was, he'd had to trade shifts with another colleague in order to get the day off.

Sandra was constantly adjusting the schedule—"to create more efficient and effective coverage," she said. It disrupted lives and child care, keeping staff off balance. Years ago, Heather had developed a system of self-scheduling. The staff worked to develop parameters for scheduling, and Heather approved them. Staff then negotiated with each other, creating staffing patterns that were best for both patients and staff. Sandra had asked that they give her a chance to see if she could improve unit operations. They didn't really have a choice.

Santos reminded herself that she and Patrick had made a pact about the night: conversation about work was off limits. Tonight was supposed to be fun. She pushed the thoughts of work out of her mind and felt the anticipation of the evening curl her lips into a smile.

Santos arrived early at Dosey Doe's Big Barn. She parked and walked into the beautiful wood-beamed structure filled with rustic Americana artifacts. The 165-year-old building, originally built in Kentucky, had originally served as a tobacco barn. Moved to Texas and rebuilt, it had become one of the most acoustically perfect music venues in the country. Big-time entertainers sought the quality and intimacy of Dosey Doe.

The universal language of music would draw about three hundred people tonight. Long tables with a charming, eclectic mix of chairs ran perpendicular to the small stage. Though nearly empty at six, the theater would soon fill with patrons sitting elbow to elbow. Strangers would become friends as they shared a meal and waited for the concert to begin. Santos always met new people here, and she was never disappointed in the food—especially the chicken-fried steak, a staple on the menu. She had saved her calories for tonight's dinner.

She had dressed with care in a long white blouse, paired with a short, vintage caramel suede fringe jacket, a long denim skirt, and her mother's Lucchese boots. A simple strand of silver Navajo pearls, a graduation gift from her parents, completed her look. She was bubbling over with excitement. Not only was this date Patrick's first time at Dosey Doe, but one of her favorite singers was performing. The country singer's spitfire style and heartrending lyrics were an authentic expression of life's sweet joys and sorrows.

Santos had always felt a deep visceral and spiritual connection with the artist's work. Music entered the brain where it not only created but recovered memories, then wrapped around the heart, and finally fed the soul. She had a hard time getting some of the melodies out of her head, like when she sang the Lorrie Morgan tune, "What Part of No." How many times had she thought of that song and smiled?

A friendly staff member walked her to their reserved seats. They were so close to the stage she could almost reach out and touch the performers. Santos watched as people entered the barn—a parade of colorful characters, all shapes and sizes, ages and attire. Seasoned cowboys walked in tall, wearing worn Stetsons, plaid shirts, and blue jeans, bulging bellies cinched tight and proud under gigantic rodeo trophy buckles. Others came dressed from work. Everyone came in search of the same thing—an escape into music, perhaps a journey back in time, the opportunity to recapture poignant memories of youth, to feel the love and longing inspired by a song and remember another time or place. Entering the barn was like passing into another dimension. Daily life, its troubles and cares, fell away.

Patrick finally arrived. She saw him right away. His eyes scanned the large room for her. *He's so handsome.* She stood up and waved both arms. He smiled and waved back, then headed her direction through the boisterous throngs of people who now filled the room.

She reached out to take his hand. "So glad you finally made it!"

"Getting a date these days is like making an appointment to see the pope or the president. Our schedules make it very complicated."

"I know," she replied. "But don't tell me about it. Time to forget about work. Let's have some fun."

"How about a kiss?"

She leaned in and hugged him, feeling his hard body. Breathing deeply, she inhaled the scent of his clean flannel shirt and light citrus aftershave. Her heart started to beat faster. She never wanted to leave the safety and warmth of his arms.

"Santos?" He pushed her away gently, holding her at arm's length. "Everything okay?"

"I'm so happy you're here. That we can share this."

Her voice trailed off.

He took her face in both his hands. She felt so small. He leaned down and kissed her tenderly. "This is just the beginning," he said. "No one will ever take this moment, this time, away from us."

The room was electric with the anticipation and energy of the crowd. Pre-concert conversation and background music filled the room.

"We'd better sit down and order," Santos said reluctantly.

They sat side by side and ordered, then introduced themselves to their neighbors across the table and on either side. It felt like a family dinner with distant relatives. One of their fellow diners entertained them with stories from his years backstage at a popular music scene. Santos had read about many of the pre-performance rituals and over-the-top, eccentric, and sometimes quirky requests of musicians—dressing rooms that contained everything from fully made beds and new toilet seats to single-color candies to cigarettes lit and ready for a quick drag during musical interludes. They laughed at the color in life and the routines and customs of musicians on the road. Santos could hardly believe some of the stories of life in the fast lane.

The master of ceremonies, in classic Western wear, climbed on the stage promptly at 8:30 p.m. After a few brief comments about the history of the barn, the great coffee, and the need for quiet during the performance, the small band energetically took the stage. The crowd roared with applause. The country star's short blonde curls hugged her head, and her eyelids sparkled with silver glitter. She had been singing since she was a child.

Santos lost herself in the music and the artistry of the performance. Every performance launched a new creative opportunity for a musician. How an artist felt one day when she performed a song could be completely different the next. The instruments they played felt and sounded different depending upon wear and weather. The synergy created by a lively, engaged audience could change the course of a concert. People who followed musicians from city to city and concert to concert experienced new music because the context and environment were always dynamic.

While Patrick's eyes stayed glued to the stage, Santos looked around the room, wondering about the audience tonight. Music affected each listener in a different way. Despite herself, she found her thoughts wandering back to work. She had done a quick study of music in preparation for the next Pathways meeting and discovered that music could stimulate the release of endorphins, powerful natural painkillers, creating an opioid-like high. She watched as couples leaned together to listen, while others sang along with the lyrics. She wondered about the life stories of every person in the audience and what drew them to Dosey Doe. As the throbbing pulse of the PA filled every corner of the room, she could feel the audience absorbing the music, becoming one with it.

The singer's occasional commentary between songs provided a glimpse into her complicated love life, the joyful and painful experiences. Her life was a colorful palette and the muse for her songs. She talked about the inspiration for one of her classic vocals and said to the audience, "Let me know if you can relate to this song."

When she launched into the country rock tune, the crowd broke into applause, whistling and howling in appreciation. Patrick and Santos had positioned their chairs so they both faced the stage. He sat behind her, his arms wrapped around her.

"She's really good," he whispered in her ear under the music.

"This would be a perfect song for Staci to sing at the party," Santos replied.

"Can she sing?"

"I think so . . . we can talk more later."

As the music pulsed through her, it became one with the rhythm of her heart. She thought about Patrick and his devotion to her. Was he too devoted? This just seemed too easy. Her love life had been anything but colorful. To listen to the musicians talk, life was a wild ride. What did she want? What did she need? Would life with Patrick be too predictable? She'd always done the right thing, taken the right path. Was she missing something? Life was fascinating and busy, but never wild—she'd never known wild. Should she? There had to be a dark side to everything. Even Patrick. Her chest tightened with angst.

As if sensing her thoughts, he leaned over her shoulder and said, "I love you."

She smiled and turned to kiss him. He cloaked her in his love. Their kiss was soft and sweet. She put aside her musings about choices and listened to the music as she soaked up his presence. The music led her heart to catalogue the memories of their love, like beads on a rosary, each one a precious pearl. He was a good man, a wonderful man. But was this the right time?

The band sang song after song, ending with the Eagles, "Love Will Keep Us Alive." Santos's eyes filled with tears. Patrick leaned forward, his breath warm on her neck. "I will always love you, no matter what." Her heart nearly broke with happiness.

STACI

The days were starting to get light earlier, but this morning, it was still dark. Staci could have lingered in bed on her day off, but staying in shape was important, and she hadn't been out for a run in a few days. Running helped keep her head clear. She slipped on sweats and worked through a routine of light stretches. Then she sat on the bed, laced up her running shoes, and reached under the pillow for her SIG Sauer. She punched the clip into place, checked that the safety was on, and tucked the gun snugly into her small-of-the-back holster, covering the bulge with her baggy T-shirt. She never ran alone in the dark.

She sprinted down the stairs of the apartment complex to the outside. In the distance, the sky was just starting to get light. The gray and black of a few puffy clouds stood out in relief against the pale pink dawn of a Gulf Coast sky. The morning was humid with the promise of spring. She inhaled deeply several times, drawing in the fragrant air—freshly cut grass, magnolia perfume, and warm earth. She rolled her shoulders to loosen up. Then she took off on a slow jog.

As she ran, she reflected. So far so good in her new life. People saw what they wanted to see. Other than a few clinical glitches Santos had noticed—and chalked up to Staci's "background" as a traveler—things were going pretty smoothly. Staci had made a habit of watching all of the health-care team, absorbing their actions, asking to practice, and studying every day. She subscribed to a free Internet service that sent her regular updates on CCU clinical topics so she was able to contribute in multidisciplinary rounds.

At the same time, her new life was having an unexpected side effect. She was getting closer and closer to the staff on the CCU. Was she living a lie? She was . . . she was lying every day. She was deceiving the people she was starting to care about—people who had welcomed her into their lives. But how could she do anything different? She was falling in love with her life, her work. She had not expected this. Now, every day, every action, drew her deeper into her dilemma. It was like a bottomless pit. There was no way to climb out. Though she finally had a family, she felt even more alone. What a paradox—she was trying to do good, trying to live a new life, and trying to make a difference, but it was all a lie.

She'd meant no harm when she started on this journey. But the more she learned, the more she realized that what she was doing was terribly wrong. It could have dangerous consequences. She was not worried so much about her own skin as she was the patients. But now there was no way out. She would live in every moment, every day until she either disappeared—probably the best option—or got caught. Not an option.

Staci pushed the dark thoughts out of her mind and focused on her breathing. She had no sense that anyone had a clue anyway—so there was nothing to worry about right now.

The area was quiet, and her feet crunched on the crushed gravel of the track that circled the blocks around Rice. Live oaks formed a canopy overhead. Rice University, known as the Ivy League School of the South, sprawled over three hundred acres in the heart of Houston. Some of the seventy buildings were architectural gems and recognized landmarks. The beauty of the landscape and the stately buildings drew photographers from all over the world.

The green eyes of a cat glowed up ahead. Staci smiled and gave the cat a wider berth. She could hear dogs barking in the distance and the occasional rain of sprinklers splashed her as she ran through the puddles. In the zone, she decided to kick it up a notch.

Her heart pounded, and she focused on deep breaths with steady, long exhales. She saw two men wearing dark hoodies jog toward her. Instinct told her to cross the street, so she did. They passed by, looking in her direction. She decided she was more comfortable keeping them in sight, so she continued her run up the block, then turned around and headed back to follow them.

A block away, she saw a woman running toward the men. As she watched, one of the men reached out, grabbed the runner around the waist, lifted her off her feet, and carried her through the high hedges. The other man followed. She heard a muffled scream, then nothing.

Adrenaline pumping, Staci ran in the direction of the woman, dodging the few cars that now populated University Boulevard. She kept her eyes on the area where she'd last seen the woman. She approached, crouched down, listening, and pulled out her gun, letting her gun arm hang at her side.

"Please don't," the woman whimpered.

"We won't hurt you," a male voice responded.

That was all the information she needed. Staci broke through the hedge. One man had the jogger down on the ground. The other stood watching.

"Let her go!"

"Look, Joey, we got two for the price of one," said the man standing.

"I don't think so." Staci raised her gun and assumed a strong firing stance, feet shoulder width apart, arms pointing toward the standing attacker, both hands locked on the gun. She moved her weight slightly forward and aimed at his chest.

He raised his hands in surrender and backed away.

"Hey, watch that gun. You could hurt someone," he said.

"I said, let her go!" Staci said loudly to the man who had the woman pinned to the ground. He did nothing. She kept her eyes and the gun pointed at the man standing. She knew she needed to call 911, but she couldn't keep her gun on the perps and call the police at the same time.

"Get off her!" she shouted. The man rolled off the woman and slowly got up. "I will shoot, make no mistake," she said. Both men started to back away.

"Got a cell phone?" she asked the girl who was now crying softly. Staci's eyes never left the men.

"Yes," she said.

"Call 911. Now!"

Staci kept the gun trained on the men. She did not want to shoot. She didn't have a permit to carry, and shooting could put her in jail—at the very least, it would break her cover. But she couldn't leave the woman until she knew she was safe.

She heard the woman start to talk to police dispatch. Then the men made a break for it. They peeled off in separate directions and ran through the hedge, out of sight. She heard a car door open and the car start. It screeched away. Catching them would be futile.

She tucked her gun back in the SOB holster. The woman was still on the ground, off her phone now, sobbing. Staci knelt down beside her.

"Everything's going to be okay . . . they're gone." In the distance, Staci could hear a police siren. "Do you need to go to the emergency room?"

The woman shook her head. She was in shock.

"I'm sure you've got some bumps and bruises," Staci said. "They didn't get your clothes off, thank God." She sighed. "Jerks."

The siren was getting louder.

"I need to stand on the street and flag them down." Staci stood up. "I'll be right back."

"Please don't leave me," the woman cried out, reaching out for Staci.

"I won't leave you. I'm not going away." She meant it.

As she stood on the curb waiting for the police, Staci worried. The gun could land her in jail. She ducked back through the hedge, crouched down next to the woman again, and said, "Say, I need to ask you to help me out. I don't have my permit to carry yet—could we not mention that I waved a gun at those guys?"

BLAKE

Gooey gossip was currency and crack for Sam. Her craving for information, the dirtier the better and the need to know all, was as strong as any addiction.

After talking with her, Blake had his first lead in a long time. Sam had reached Staci, but she was only able to get one tidbit of information—Staci was working in Houston in or near the Texas Medical Center. He probed Sam for more, and she prattled on and on about Staci and her new life in Houston, but he doubted much of it. Sam didn't know the difference between fact and fiction, sometimes exaggerating stories to increase the value of her information while puffing up her self-esteem with smoke. *Mistake number one: don't ever tell Sam anything you don't want the world to know. Staci blew it. Why? She knows better.*

Blake had been in town a few days, cruising the metro area, getting the lay of the land, picking up a woman here and there. He found the Houston bar scene vibrant and colorful. He loved the combination of Southern women and Western chic. The guys he met described a true Southern woman as an iron fist in a velvet glove. The gals ranged from young and reckless to aging steel magnolias hungry for a brief adventure. The scene was a lot more sophisticated than he'd expected. But people everywhere liked to drink, hook up, and have fun. Houston was no different. He loved the challenge and anonymity. He was the invisible man; he could blend in and disappear. His drugged conquests would never remember him. He made sure of that.

The giant Houston Livestock and Rodeo Show had

just ended, and the town was still juiced with energy. It was early, but he had no place to go, so he found a seat in a small bar downtown. It was quiet, just a few patrons sitting at the long oak bar, a beat-up relic rescued from demolition. He was taking the night off from the hunt. He wondered where Staci would hang out. There were no bars in the Medical Center area.

The flat-screen TV, recessed in an arched niche above rows and rows of assorted colorful liquor bottles, was tuned to the evening news. The news anchor, one hot babe, was worth watching. She was reporting a story about a woman jogger who was saved from rape.

"This morning Staci Stevens, a nurse from the Texas Medical Center, out for an early morning run in the West University area, rescued a fellow jogger."

For a second, the video showed a tall blonde with short hair. She put out her hand to block the camera and walked away.

Blake sat up, electrified.

Whoa—was that—could it be—his Staci?

"The woman who was attacked didn't wish to be identified." They were showing the woman's legs and jogging shoes. The reporter continued, "She said that the heroine came out of nowhere, and her attackers fled. Police found the attackers' car abandoned in a convenience store parking lot."

A nurse? Staci a nurse! That must be a mistake. Maybe the other jogger was a nurse. Got to call Sam!

PATRICK

"If I were not a physicist, I would probably be a musician.
I often think in music.
I live my daydreams in music.
I see my life in terms of music."
Albert Einstein

Patrick grabbed a cup of strong, stale coffee in the lounge. His stomach rumbled with hunger, and he searched everywhere for a snack. There was nothing on the counter but a few crumbs. The refrigerator was full of labeled lunches and expired yogurt containers. What was that smell? *Disgusting!* He hunted through the bags and containers and found a piece of runny, moldy cheese stuck in the back. He tossed the yogurt and the cheese in the trash. He was striking out. *Nothing—not a crumb.*

When Emma and Heather were around, the unit was always well supplied with homemade treasures—everything from muffins and cookies to the occasional gumbo. They were not just great leaders, but wonderful cooks who shared the bounty of their lives and homes with their work family. He sorely missed them. So did everyone else. Their absence made the unit seem lost, in a vacuum, void of the colors of their personalities. He missed Emma's down-to-earth attitude, her humor, and her maternal way of wrapping you in her arms and making you feel like everything would be okay. She was his go-to person for clinical issues and ethical questions. Heather was a paradox. Warm yet reserved, she taught them what they needed to know, gave them developmental opportunities, then let them go and grow. She'd said to him one day when giving him an important assignment, "I'll let you trip and fall, but I won't let you break a leg."

His mind was clicking away at high speed when he walked into the conference room for the Pathways task force meeting. Nick, Mary, Staci, Richard, and Santos were already gathered. He stopped. Something was different.

Kathleen and Kamy walked in talking. They paused in midsentence.

Beethoven's Ninth Symphony played in the background. The music washed over them in exciting then soothing waves. The classical piece triggered a strong visceral memory, beautiful yet melancholy, exhilarating him. His mind traveled back to another moment in time. He had not thought about it in years.

Everyone was quiet as the music continued.

Nick had brought in small, portable, high-quality speakers with a docking station. Music was playing from his smartphone in preparation for this task force meeting. Nick grinned at Patrick as if to say, "Gotcha."

"Come on in, everybody," Nick said. "I want to hear first impressions, then we're going to run you through some music drills."

Kamy jumped in first. "Stopped me in my tracks. Felt as if my blood pressure dropped."

"Lost track immediately of where I was," Kamy added.

Patrick's bittersweet memory still stirred in his heart, and he looked at Santos, who smiled, encouraging him to speak. "Surfaced something I haven't thought about for years. When I first heard that symphony, I was with my father. It was the first time I'd ever been to a Houston Symphony Orchestra concert. I really didn't want to go, but Dad insisted. He was so wise. I loved it. It was so beautiful, I got lost in the music. It was a special father-son moment that I will always treasure. We went out to dinner afterwards and talked and talked. Dad was healthy—in good shape. I had no clue he would die so suddenly the next month." Patrick looked down at his hands.

"So in this moment, with one piece of music, we have three different reactions," Nick said.

"Music is experienced differently by all people. It's very personal, intimate even," Mary said.

"Let's try another experiment with music," Nick continued. He went over to his phone and scrolled down to another selection. Ravel's "Bolero" began to play.

"*Ten*—it reminds me of the movie!" Santos jumped in.

"What's that?" Kathleen asked. "I've never heard of it."

Patrick knew the one. "You might never have seen it— it's a classic with Dudley Moore, Julie Andrews, and Bo Derek."

Mary guided the group down another path. "Think about the music you hear in stores. How does it make you feel?"

"Sometimes it makes me want to leave," Santos said with a laugh. "If it's too loud, not my style, or abrasive. Makes me want to get out as quickly as possible."

Patrick nodded. "The same thing goes for me in restaurants. If the music is too loud, it pushes me away. Stresses me out. Why do they need music in restaurants?"

"I love walking into a store and being hit by the beat of hot music," Kamy said. "Makes me want to shop. Stay and listen. Dance in the clothes I'm looking at. Think about how I could wear them—where to wear them."

"What we're seeing here is how the impact of music is filtered by generational differences, personal preferences, and memories—as well as the quality of the sound and the setting," Richard said. "Music surrounds us. We play music in the OR. Surgeons have preferences. Sometimes we ask patients what kind of music they would like to hear during surgery."

"Dentists have been offering headphones to patients to reduce dental anxiety for decades," Santos added. "I never want to use them. Like to know what's going on in my mouth." The group laughed. She smiled sheepishly at Patrick. *Learning more about her every day. Didn't know about her dental anxiety.*

"Music is a powerful force in the human experience. It's been used in labor and delivery, creating a soothing environment when the mother selects the music for the birth of the child—producing healthier outcomes. Some hospitals have brought musicians, violinists, into units such as telemetry, and the patient response has been tremendous."

Patrick spoke with the passion he felt, heightened by last night's time at Dosey Doe and the memories Nick had stirred with his opening music. He'd been giving a lot of thought to the purpose of Pathways, and the emotion awakened by the music just underscored it. "Life is so multifaceted. Yet we strip it down when patients enter the hospital. We strip them of their clothes, their family support, their jewelry, and we hook them up to machines that have alarms and beep all night. We feed them bland, cold food in plastic containers. At a time when they need to embrace the simple comforts and joys of being human, we take it all away from them. This could add another dimension back to patients and give them choices, soothe their spirits, bond families around familiar music that has meaning to them."

Richard spoke up. "There is actually quite a bit of research on the impact of music on clinical practice, and a professional organization devoted to it. The International Association for Music and Medicine has been around for quite some time. They have a journal and regular conferences. Yet very few clinicians, unless you are a musician," Richard smiled, "consider how to weave music into patient care. In addition, there is Center for Music and End of Life Care. It has a great deal of information on using music as a clinical resource. We've posted all of this on our unit intranet website. I'd encourage you all to take a look."

"So the bottom line here is, how should we integrate music into the care of our Pathways patients in a way that actually makes a difference?" Nick said.

"Before we can answer that, I think everyone needs time to study and digest this information," Santos said.

"Maybe we should create a checklist, or ask the patients, just randomly, what kind of music they like," Staci offered. "Considering most of them are older, it might be classical music."

Richard chimed in, "Music from the '40s and '50s can be quite powerful for people of this generation. During WWII, when Dad was in the Navy on a ship in the Pacific, the officers would broadcast big-band music over the PA while the guys were working on the deck. It helped them feel less homesick. We might even ask patients to come up with a list of tunes, and we can create a playlist for them. We can help them load it on their smartphone and they can listen during procedures that might be uncomfortable, or just play the music to create periods of relaxation. And since we are already overstimulated in the CCU, we should again be conscious of lights—turning them off at night, keeping our voices quiet at night, and generally keeping noise to a minimum."

"Another thing we could do is remind family members to bring in headphones or earbuds to listen to music," Kamy offered.

"Remember to think about the continuum of care," Richard added. "Some music might be appropriate for rest, some for sleep or distraction during procedures—other music might be played as the patient is close to death. Don't think about music for just one purpose. And keep in mind that music's effect isn't all positive—it could potentially ease depression, yet it can also create melancholy."

Richard's comment sparked another poignant memory. "I get that," Patrick said. "Mother used to cry when she heard a song that they used to dance to. It was bittersweet to hear the music—happy memories, but sad that Dad was gone. But expression of feelings is often healing—in the right environment. Wouldn't you agree?"

Heads nodded.

Nick continued. "This is complicated, but it should be an interesting topic to follow up. Okay, Staci, why don't you take the lead and work with Kamy and Kathleen to query the patients and come up with a list of tunes?"

"You can count on me for the titles of tunes from almost any era," Richard offered. "I have a lot of music on CDs and on vinyl. We can always digitize the vinyl."

"You know, sometimes the volunteers have a slush fund to buy small items for the units. We might be able to get some support from them if our patients don't have their own devices to play music," Mary said.

"Great idea," Santos replied. "Can you follow through on that, Mary?"

"Sure can."

"Okay, we've got some work to do before the next meeting. But we need to make sure we've got all of the right patients on our current Pathways list. I know everyone has gone off in different directions with their patients, and this is taking a little bit longer to get completely organized, but I think we have a good idea of who they are," Santos continued.

"We definitely have Mrs. Cartwright, Mrs. Scalina, and Mr. Hope-Simon on the list," Nick said.

"Both Mr. Hope-Simon and Mrs. Cartwright are well on their Pathway. We need to add music therapy to their plan of care," Santos said.

Patrick couldn't help thinking about the McIntire family. He was haunted by Mr. McIntire's death. A peaceful passing had turned traumatic with CPR. Though the family had not been ready to join the Pathways program, he had died in the worst possible situation—CPR when there was no hope. Patrick felt as if he had failed. He had been unable to assure them that there was a better way to die.

He spoke up. "I really wish we could have convinced the McIntire family to join the Pathways movement. Maybe if we had introduced them to some of the positives of music, even though they weren't on the list, it might have opened up their thoughts and emotions about dying. Am I hoping too much? I just can't seem to let this one go."

Staci smiled at him. "Patrick, I think you did everything you could. Sometimes people need more time to find their way. It was their decision, not yours. Death is a path we take alone, no matter how much support we have—and you only do it once."

Patrick was touched by the wisdom of Staci's words. "You're right. All the more important that we help." He looked at Santos, and her eyes were warm with understanding.

"Staci, have you started with Mrs. Scalina yet? Do you need some help?" Santos asked.

"We've talked, but not in an organized way. I could use some guidance in this area. I've never done this before."

"No problem. We're all learning."

"Hey, Staci—not to change subjects," Nick interrupted, "but were you out jogging the other day—interrupted a potential rape? Nancy was off and thought she saw you on the six o'clock news."

Patrick's brain buzzed with questions and a few concerns. "Staci? Where were you?"

She shrugged it off. "It was nothing. I was on my usual circuit, spotted two guys—actually thought they might be trailing me. So I avoided them, then doubled back—caught them dragging this young woman through the bushes around Rice. I yelled at them—told them I was an undercover cop. Guess I just scared them away."

Patrick glanced over at Santos, and their eyes met in understanding. She had told him about Staci's gun. He hoped she hadn't been carrying when she ran into the thugs. Guns were dangerous, even when you thought you knew how to handle them. It was two against one, and she should have realized they might be armed. If they'd gotten control of her gun—he dreaded the thought—they might not be having this conversation.

"Staci, please be careful," Santos said.

"I know what I did was dangerous. But I couldn't help myself. I wasn't going to allow her to be raped." Staci paused, and Patrick got the sense that the incident had surfaced memories of her own—heavy memories. "If every person who saw a potential crime in action stepped up to the plate—helped each other out—maybe the world would be a better place. I had to take that risk."

"Well, everything worked out okay—this time. Staci, be careful. You're tough and smart, and though this area is usually safe, we have our share of crime." Patrick sighed and tucked the conversation in the back of his mind for future reference. He felt a brotherly concern for Staci that had grown as he watched Santos and Staci become closer. He didn't like the thought of her playing vigilante.

"Never a dull moment around here. Let's get back to work, everyone. We have patients who need us."

SANTOS

Santos left the meeting worried about Staci. It took a lot of courage to do what she'd done—she just hoped that Staci had not threatened the men with her gun. *Does she have a Texas permit to carry?* She could lose her nursing license if convicted of a felony. Staci probably hadn't even thought, just reacted to the threat. Santos had noticed that Staci had a very high adjustment level—she stayed calm in a crisis. The personality attribute was essential for a successful critical care nurse.

Santos had been working with Mrs. Cartwright to create transitional plans for her Pathway since their first conversation. The elderly woman had made decisions and signed a living will; a copy was in the electronic patient record. She had a DNR order and was the first person on the unit and in the hospital to follow the Allow Natural Death plan of care. It was time for her to go home to die. She was stabilized, and though she might have weeks to months to live, she did not want to return to the hospital under any circumstances. Santos was relieved, yet sad. She had crossed the path of a strong woman with incredible wisdom and character. Once again, Santos was learning about life through her patients. She would miss her greatly.

She walked toward her patient thinking of what they had learned about music. She'd get Mrs. Cartwright up in the chair again, and they could have one of their chats.

As she approached the bed, she saw that Mrs. Cartwright was asleep. She walked over and quickly looked up at the monitor. There was no heart rhythm displayed—but no alarm. Then she remembered—they had turned off the sound to allow her to rest. Maybe a monitor lead had come off?

She stood next to the bed and checked Mrs. Cartwright's pulse. Her hand was cold. There was no pulse. She put her hand under her nose. She could feel no air movement. Mrs. Cartwright was not breathing. Santos's heart pounded. She took out her stethoscope and listened for a heartbeat—nothing.

Santos walked quickly back to the hallway. Nick was standing there talking with Staci.

"Nick, could you come here please?" Santos asked. Her heart was heavy.

Nick came over and followed her to Mrs. Cartwright's bedside.

"I think she's gone," Santos told him.

Nick took out his stethoscope and mirrored Santos's actions. No heartbeat. Then he took out his reflex hammer, uncovered Mrs. Cartwright's foot, and stroked the soles of her feet looking for an a response. There was none. He tried one more reflex—nothing.

"Santos, you're right. She's gone. I'm sorry," Nick said. He reached over to grasp Santos across the shoulders and gave her an encouraging squeeze. "I know you cared a lot about her."

"Thanks, Nick. I'm sorry too. She was a lovely person. I'm just so sorry that she didn't get to go home—that she had to die here, and alone. I hope she didn't suffer in any way."

"She looks peaceful, as if she just passed in her sleep," Nick offered.

"I hope so." Santos felt grief welling up, her heart once

again breaking from the loss of someone very special—someone she had cared about. The unexpectedness of it threatened to knock her off balance.

"We did our best, Santos. It was her time. But I know it's never easy."

Santos shook her head, her eyes filling with tears. "Nick, can you declare her? I'll look up the family information and have them come in to see her. Her children are going to be very upset—not just that she died, but that she died here, alone. They were so happy to help her die on her terms, at home. They worked so hard to get everything ready."

She stopped to cover Mrs. Cartwright's feet. Then she opened the bedside table drawers to look for a clean nightgown. "I wonder who'll take her dog?" Santos muttered, thinking out loud. "Gosh, I hate making these calls. But they all know me, so it won't be a stranger calling. I always wonder what to say. I need to say a little prayer that I find the right words. I'll ask Staci to help me get her ready for a visit—maybe Patrick can take my other patient. I'll get Chaplain Smith here to pray with the family. We'll bathe her, then dress her in one of her pretty nightgowns before the family arrives."

BLAKE

Blake caught up with Sam a few hours after the story broke. He told her about the television report where he had learned that Staci was posing as "Staci Stevens." On mission, sure that he was close, Blake asked Sam if she could search for more information. Sam quickly went into action. Since Staci had never called her back, Sam was not only annoyed but suspicious, and more than happy to help.

Blake's patience was quickly rewarded. Sam searched the Internet using Staci Stevens and found a recently posted YouTube video. She sent him the link, and he was able to view it on his phone.

He couldn't believe his eyes. It was a smartphone video of a group of musicians rehearsing songs, uploaded by some guy named Nick. In the narrative, he included the names of everyone. One of the people in the video was Staci. He'd had no idea she could sing. It ended with a tall young man approaching the camera and saying, "We hope you can join us at Mother's on Saturday night. Celebrate the biggest moment of my life!"

The video ended. He watched it over and over, his rage building to a crescendo.

The timing was perfect. Saturday night the CCU would be quiet, the census low, and the youngsters on duty. She would be long gone and have the perfect alibi.

One of the Pathway patients, Michael Hope-Simon, was scheduled to go home Monday. They were waiting for hospice to replace his bed with a hospital bed. The staff loved him. He was so grateful for their assistance, a gentleman in every way. He had lived a rich international life and had many stories to tell. They found his English accent enchanting and talked with him constantly about the series they all enjoyed, Downton Abbey.

His wife was anxious about caring for him at home, yet she wanted him to feel safe and surrounded by loved ones. She had reassured her that hospice nurses would provide tremendous support and that he would find great comfort being at home and would finally get some sleep. She had sent Mrs. Hope-Simon home for some rest.

Since it was the weekend, she had to the keys to all of the pumps. She opened the pump to access the controls. Adjusting the morphine drip took a few seconds, and she chatted with Mr. Hope-Simon, patting his arm, straightening his bed, tucking him in for an afternoon nap. The cumulative effect of the drug would occur long after she was gone. Slipping into a coma would not be a bad way to go. It might not be on his terms, but it would be on hers.

STACI

It was one of those perfect spring days in Houston. The live oaks' new leaves shimmered yellow-green in the sun. After an unseasonably cold winter, the snapdragons were finally going crazy with tall spikes of multicolored blooms, while sweet alyssum and jasmine perfumed the breeze. Pollen, thick as cornmeal, covered everything with a pale green dust.

Living on the edge was becoming an everyday habit. Her life was beautiful, satisfying, and fun. Today was a very special day. Once again she pushed her feelings of guilt down deep inside and put herself in character for another great ride. She could not remember a more gorgeous day or a time she'd felt more excited. She looked at herself in the car mirror. Pumped with the adrenaline of anticipation, her cheeks were flushed, and her eyes sparkled with excitement.

Smiling, she parked in the back lot and walked quickly around the building to the huge, roughhewn double doors of Mother's. Rumor had it that one of the bar's owners was musician Lyle Lovett. He called Klein, Texas, home. *Wonder if he's ever here?* She pushed the heavy doors open, her eyes adjusting to the near darkness. The place was quiet and empty. She inhaled and smelled leather, wood, and beer. Peanut shells cracked underfoot. She took a deep breath and looked around the quiet room, letting the ambience wrap around her, absorbing the setting and looking forward to the evening ahead.

The bar was a huge architectural semicircle. Tiered

rows of tables and chairs, also in a semicircle, bordered the bar, reaching nearly three stories high. Seamless wrap-around video screens surrounded the slightly elevated center stage. The karaoke and video equipment was state of the art. Microphones, amplifiers, and a set of drums were already on stage. A generous, well-worn dance floor circled the platform. *It's perfect.*

She had splurged on her costume. A black suede vest, delicately embroidered with gold beads hit her at mid-thigh. Cascades of fringe swung with every move. Slim blue jeans and boots completed her look. She smiled. Tonight was the night.

They had been rehearsing now for days, separately. It had been a challenge to find the time with work so daunting. Practice was a refuge from the trauma of work, the deaths, the drama, the conflict. It was through the music that they found respite. Though she was about the same age as her clinical colleagues, she felt so much older. She lived in a parallel universe to their world and had only joined them because she wore a disguise and played a part—a part that was becoming as close to her as her own skin. They had welcomed her into their hearts and lives. And they had included her in this new adventure when the team of clinicians joyfully conspired to become a group of musicians. Their goal was to celebrate life and the engagement of Nick and Nancy.

Richard, Santos, Nick, Melissa, and Staci were the main event. The team of performers had only one rehearsal together on the weekend. Nick had downloaded music videos and created photo streams to run during the songs. He had orchestrated everything, an engagement surprise for Nancy. He thought he was the only one who knew the plan, but Staci knew differently. She felt a little wicked knowing more than the party planner. But she was good at keeping secrets. She had to be.

The doors flew open, and Nick rushed in.

"I'm late—Staci, can you help me with these things?" Nick was carrying bags of music and CDs. "I told Nancy to wait in the car. She's suspicious. She knows me too well."

Richard Whiting walked in. Staci did a double take.

His long white hair hung free—no ponytail tonight. His green eyes sparkled with mischief; gold aviator sunglasses perched on his nose. No signature white lab coat. He wore faded blue jeans torn at the knees, a well-worn T-shirt that said "Rolling Stones," and a beat-up brown leather bomber jacket. He carried a worn guitar case.

"Dr. Whiting?" Staci sputtered.

A lovely, tall brunette with long brown hair stood behind Richard. She threw her head back and laughed. The sound was richly melodic and knowing. Staci regarded her with interest, and wondered who the babe with Richard was.

"Staci, we're playing in a band tonight. Cut me some slack."

The woman with Richard reached out her hand to Staci. "Hi, I'm Julie . . . his wife of forty years. Nurse and former groupie." She smiled warmly, and her eyes sparkled.

Staci and Nick both shook Julie's hand. Staci thought she was stunning. Julie glowed with love. Her sense of humor was palpable. Staci looked back and forth between Richard and his wife. They looked so different, but their connection was electric.

"My love, you were never a groupie."

Richard turned to Nick. "I think the cat's out of the bag. Nancy saw us as we were heading in. You'd better collect your fiancée from the car or she'll never forgive you."

Nick pushed the equipment at Staci, who shouldered the bags.

"Give those to me . . . I'll take them up there," Richard said. "I've got to do a sound check. Honey, can you take my guitar?" Staci handed off the bags to Richard as Julie picked up the guitar case. "Oh, Honey, will you take a look at the stage door and make sure it's unlocked?" Julie nodded and headed toward the stage.

Staci felt awkward, uncertain what to say to her medical director turned musician.

"Sorry, Dr. Whiting, I knew you played in bands, but I've never seen you looking like this."

"It's okay, Staci," he smiled. "You look the part yourself."

She laughed, relieved. "Thanks, never did this part before."

"You'll do great. You have talent." Staci's heart leaped with the compliment. He smiled and put his hand on her shoulder, then walked away in the direction of his wife.

The door swung open again, lighting the dim room. Particles of dust and pollen danced in the sunlight of early evening. Staci turned around as Patrick and Santos walked in. His arm was draped around Santos's shoulders. Eyes on Santos, he asked, "So are you going to tell me now?"

Santos's laugh was joyful and teasing. "Not yet. It's a surprise. Isn't it, Staci?"

Staci's heart warmed at the sight of the couple, and at the shared secret with Santos. These people were truly her friends—almost her family. "Yes, it's a surprise . . . but not for long."

"Wow, look at you, Staci! You look fantastic! You could almost be *her!*" Santos untangled herself from Patrick and walked over to finger the beads on Staci's vest. "This is a beauty. Turn around . . . let me get the whole effect. Did you get this during the rodeo? It's gorgeous!"

Staci twirled around, laughing. The fringe on her vest swirled around her. "You look great yourself," Staci replied. She knew all about Santos's Lucchese boots. Now she admired the antique cream blouse, decorated at the sleeves and hem with tablecloth lace, the intricately crafted silver and turquoise studded concha belt, and the long denim skirt.

"Where did you get that?" Staci touched the beautiful belt.

"It's a loaner . . . from my sister Maria."

"Very cool. Did Camilla make you this blouse? I know you really admired the one she made for herself."

"Sure did. You have a good memory."

"I'm a pretty good listener," Staci replied.

The door opened again, and everyone turned around. The sun was setting, and the two couples who entered were backlit against the sky. Staci raised her hand, shielding her eyes from the blinding sun.

"Emma!" Santos cried out. "Heather! I didn't know you were coming! I don't know which one of you to hug first!" Emma and Heather and their husbands, Leon and Don, walked in to a chorus of greetings.

Staci stepped back. She had never met either of these two women, yet she felt she knew them. The unit never stopped talking about them. They were legends. She felt a little out of place and alone. She watched Santos run and first crush Emma, and then reach out more carefully for Heather.

"How did you know about this?" Santos asked.

"Richard told us," Emma replied.

"I'm so glad you came!" Santos said and gave Heather another hug.

"We wouldn't miss it for the world," Heather said. "My counts were good enough that I could be out in public. Miss you all so much. Plus, I needed a bit of a distraction." She looked over at her husband and smiled lovingly. "Don did too."

Santos turned to Staci. "Staci, this is perfect. Come meet Emma and Heather."

Heather, her head covered by a wide-brimmed, rust-colored straw hat, reached out with both of her hands to clasp Staci's. "So glad to finally meet you. I hear you're doing really well on the unit." Her hands were warm and dry and Staci felt an immediate connection.

Yet Staci didn't know what to say. *What do you say to someone who is going through chemotherapy and has lost her hair?*

"Thank you, Heather. It's wonderful to meet you. You have a great team." Staci paused to search for the right words. "I love your hat."

"Why, thank you." Heather reached up to reposition the hat, which had slipped with the hugs. "Some of my friends gave me a hat shower, right when 'curing therapy' started. This is one of my favorites." Heather gave Staci a big smile and looked at her kindly with peaceful blue eyes. Staci's heart warmed even as part of her wanted to panic. If her secret was ever found out, she didn't think Heather's eyes would be so welcoming.

"And this is Emma." Santos grabbed Staci by the hand and dragged her over to a beautiful woman with skin the color of milk chocolate and a head of tight black curls. Emma appraised her with wise, deep brown eyes, and reached her hand out.

"Glad to finally meet you, Staci. I've heard good things."

"Emma—this is such a surprise! Where's your Western wear?" Santos asked.

"Honey, no way it would fit on this body." Emma looked down and stretched out her hands. "Look at me! No, I take that back! Don't look at me. I've gained so much weight taking care of Mama. I'm going to have to stop cooking, go on Weight Watchers, do something . . . or I won't fit into my scrubs." Emma went on to explain that she was in Houston for the weekend and probably wouldn't be back for another few weeks.

The bar was starting to fill with Saturday night customers. The team of clinicians moved away from the doors, and Nick and Nancy managed to slip in with the crowd.

"What's going on here? I'm confused," Nancy asked.

The tall, slim blonde was not wearing scrubs tonight. Staci thought she looked gorgeous in her Western wear. Nancy wore a black cowboy hat that created a lovely contrast with her shoulder-length, light blonde hair. The anesthesiologist had dressed all in black except for a pink scarf around her neck. A rhinestone belt circled her tiny waist. Staci knew from experience that Nancy was not only beautiful but incredibly bright.

"Just a few more minutes, Honey, and I'll tell you," Nick responded. "Let's go to our table."

Nancy looked at him through narrowed eyes but turned to follow him.

"I guess I'll see ya'll later," she said over her shoulder as she sauntered away, shaking her head.

Taking Nick's lead, Santos said, "We'd better sit down." She took Patrick by one hand, Emma by the other, and pulled. "Come on, everyone!"

Staci followed, feeling awkward and trying to regain her sense of confidence and belonging. They found their reserved seats, center stage, midway up the tiered bar.

Nick took the stage. He tapped the microphone a couple of times and was rewarded with loud metallic clicks.

"Good evening, everyone! Thank you for coming. We've planned a special celebration tonight . . . to celebrate a special engagement. I can't believe I'm actually saying this—I found the love of my life! And we're getting married!"

The crowd of people from the CCU and strangers in the audience clapped and stomped.

"Nancy, I love you!" Nick shouted into the mike. "Will you please stand up so people can see the gorgeous, brilliant, talented, wonderful woman who has agreed to marry me?"

The crowd hooted and hollered again. Nancy stood up and gave the crowd a prom-queen wave.

"Well, since this is a mixed crowd, we're only going to take over the stage for a while, and then the rest of you in the audience are welcome to come up and sing. We hope you'll join along." Nick looked behind him and motioned to an overhead screen while he explained, "We'll run the lyrics of most of the songs on the screen here."

Staci took her eyes off Nick and looked around the room to gauge the interest of the audience. From her perch above center stage, she noticed two men enter the bar. They were dressed in jeans and boots, but one was wearing a long leather duster—a little warm for the evening—and the other a sport coat. *They must be carrying.* One of the men walked to the bar and leaned against it, then turned around and scanned the room. The other stood by the door and studied the bar carefully. They looked like they fit in, but they were more interested in the crowd than the stage. That seemed odd.

The security team has arrived, she told herself. She was really excited now, but that quickly escalated into nervousness. Her palms started to sweat, and she rubbed them dry on her jeans. She had never met professional musicians before, much less performed with them. Nick was about to be blown away by the surprise Richard had arranged. Staci hoped she could find her voice when the time came to sing.

Santos leaned over to Staci. "I'm really starting to get nervous now . . . I've never done this before."

"You'll do great. You're a natural, and your song is perfect for your voice," Staci reassured her.

"If you think so." Santos sighed and turned to focus on the stage. "I haven't sung in public since choir in high school."

"It's time!" Staci nudged Santos. "Get ready. It's your turn."

Staci gave Santos an encouraging hug as Nick boomed from the stage.

"We hope you can all relate to the songs we're going to do tonight. We're going to start out slow with a love song sung by one of our favorite nurses, Santos!" Nick shaded his eyes from the spotlight and looked for Santos.

Santos walked up the stairs to the stage, gave Nick a hug, and took the mike.

"I'm going to sing a song written by Randy Newman and pretty much immortalized by Bonnie Raitt. Some of you might have seen the movie *Michael,* where an angel, played by John Travolta, comes back to earth to experience the joys of life. This song was in that movie." Santos looked behind her to Melissa, who, dressed in her "rock star" costume of black sequined jeans and a bright pink suede jacket with a pink cowboy hat, was at the piano. Melissa nodded and began the quiet introduction of "Feels Like Home to

Me." Nick on drums and Richard on guitar would back her up.

As Santos sang the love song, Staci's eyes pricked with tears. She watched a tear slide down Patrick's face as he listened to the poignant ballad beautifully sung by Santos. The song was over quickly, and Santos bowed to the applause, smiled broadly with relief, and blew kisses to the crowd who applauded and hollered, "More! More!" Santos bowed again and walked off the stage.

Nick kept the show going, quickly taking the mike again. Richard walked up to him. *It was time.* Nick looked confused as Richard reached over and took the microphone. Guitar in hand, Richard said, "Slight change in plans, Nick. I hope you don't mind, but a few old friends stopped by to join us tonight. After all, it's a pretty special night for all of us. We get to celebrate—enjoy, and have fun together." Richard smiled and signaled to Julie, who stood on the side of the stage.

Nick backed away, confused and speechless as he tried to figure out what was going on.

Richard spoke into the microphone. "Folks, it's time to rev it up with some rock!" The crowd cheered. "So, without further ado . . ." Richard strummed a few C chords to begin the 1, 4, 5 classic rock progression, the prelude to a song of blues-based boogie rock, ". . . I'd like to introduce some of the members of a little rock band from Texas . . ." The crowd jumped to their feet, screaming.

The music video to ZZ Top's "Gimme All Your Lovin'" started to play on the surround-sound screens and two well-known and loved professional musicians entered from backstage. Nick raced to his drums to begin the intro to the tune he had practiced but had no idea he'd be playing with such musical icons. Nancy got up and screamed with joy. She grabbed Staci by the hand, and they ran down the tiered steps of the bar to the dance floor. They were quickly joined by Santos and Patrick as well as a dozen other assorted couples. The crowd sang along at the chorus—everyone knew the words. When the song ended, the crowd roared and stomped for more.

Richard took the mike again and looked back at Nick at the drums. He flashed a huge grin at Nick, who was dripping with sweat. Nick wiped his face with a towel and hung it around his neck, shaking his head and smiling wryly at Richard. The rest of the band grabbed sips of water, chatted quietly, and waited.

Richard's voice boomed over the PA again. "We're going to introduce a new singer to you tonight, but you'll all recognize the song."

Suddenly Staci felt dizzy. Her heart pounded, and her hands started to shake.

"Knock 'em dead!" Santos whispered. "Get on up there. If I can do it, you can do it! Come on, girl. Move it!"

Staci smiled weakly. Her feet felt frozen to the ground. She was more terrified than she'd ever been in her life. *So this is stage fright.*

Melissa ran down the steps to the dance floor, grabbed Staci by the hand, and dragged her up onto the stage.

"Come on. I'll start it with you. It's a great song!" Melissa looked Staci directly in the eyes. "Come on . . . you know this song."

Melissa turned and motioned to Nick to lead into the song. Nick began the classic country drumbeat, and the rest of the band started to play the intro of the Lorrie Morgan song, "Cleanin' Out My Closet." Staci started softly, then got into the spirited rhythm, found her voice, and began to strut back and forth across the stage. Melissa laughed and headed back to play keyboards. Pictures and videos of Nick and Nancy streamed across the screens behind the performers. The audience got into the lyrics and sang along with Staci.

As soon as the song ended, Richard on lead guitar got the crowd's attention with the signature long staccato E intro to the Heart classic "Barracuda." The crowd roared its approval. Staci nailed the song, and the crowd jumped to their feet, clapping and whistling. She bowed and quickly left the stage.

"I think I know what an MI feels like," she said as she sat down next to Santos. Staci's heart beat as fast as a burst of tachycardia. Santos passed her a glass of water. Staci took a long drink and sat back in her chair.

"You were amazing!" Santos said.

Staci was thrilled, swept away by the music, the crowd, the feeling of being one with the music. She was high with the euphoria of success.

The time had passed so quickly. They had one more song to do, and that song belonged to Nick.

Richard approached the microphone one last time. "I want to thank my dear friends from old times, for joining us tonight." The crowd erupted and jumped to their feet. "We have one more song to do—sung by our future groom for his future bride. The song is by the Eagles, 'Love Will Keep Us Alive.' Nick?"

As Nick thanked everyone for listening and joining in, the stage went dark, with all but a spotlight on Nick. Staci noticed the celebrities quietly leaving the stage, leaving Richard, Melissa, and Nick alone. They melted into the darkness, escaping before the crowd realized they were gone. She scanned the bar for the security team. They were gone as well.

Nick sang the song with great passion. As Staci looked around the room at the couples who sat together, sharing a kiss or a long look, she wondered if she would ever find a love like Santos and Patrick or Nick and Nancy. Tears filled her eyes. Santos looked over at Staci, seemed to read her feelings, and reached over to give her a hug.

⌁

Later that night, Staci left Nick and Nancy in the bar and headed out to her car. It was dark, but the stars were out and the air was cool with a hint of humidity. *What a great night—the best night of my life.* Staci replayed the evening in her head, rolling over the details, smiling all the way. They were all such great people—so talented and so dedicated. She felt so blessed.

She took out the keys to her car and pressed the remote unlock.

"Was that song about you . . . or about me?" a male voice called from behind her. Staci stopped dead. She knew that voice. On this warm, humid night, it turned her hands to ice.

She turned around slowly.

A cigarette glowed in the darkness and then died. Blake emerged from the shadows. He took his time walking toward her. The night was quiet. The crunch of his boots on the gravel was the only sound in the empty parking lot. He kept his eyes on her as he walked and smiled. That smile used to take her breath away. Now it turned her cold. He stopped within a foot of her. Then he flicked his cigarette to the ground and crushed it into the gravel with the toe of his boot. Blake's every movement had purpose.

Her heart pounded. *How did he find me?* What would

he do?

She was speechless. His powerful body towered over her. He was bigger than she remembered.

"It's good to see you, Darlin' . . . I've been looking for you for months. I've missed you." His voice was sweet and low, like a lover.

"I didn't see you in there . . . I didn't know you were there," Staci replied. "How did you find me?"

"Got a tip, followed it up . . . saw the whole show. It was quite a show. Didn't know you could sing like that— very, very sexy, Darlin'."

He moved closer. His index finger slowly traced along her jawline, following her neck, down to her breasts. She could smell his body. She remembered that scent. Her head flooded with memories. Her heart pounded. She wondered what was next.

He withdrew his hand and stepped back, giving her body a long look, his eyes resting on her breasts.

"You're looking really good . . . better than ever."

He raked her body with his eyes, taking his time, savoring her every curve. His eyes, simmering with lust, invaded hers. She felt as vulnerable as if she were standing naked before him.

"Why don't you and I go somewhere and catch up?"

Though Staci had mentally prepared for this possibility, she was caught off guard by her body's reflex reaction to his look and touch. The physical response was a shock. It bypassed her brain. It had been a long time since she'd been with anyone. The sense of longing nearly swept her away. She had not been touched or held by a man in months. He had always been hard to resist.

"How about it, Darlin'?"

Blake gently pushed her against the car and guided his

hard body against her. She could feel the Glock he always carried. She turned her head away, and he kissed her neck. His lips were soft and warm. Desire flowed through her with every beat of her heart. She was alone. She wanted him. He wanted her. *What would it hurt?*

Her mind flashed back on her dark past. The mistakes she'd made. The mistakes she wanted to leave behind. She was a runaway. Survival meant continuing to run.

I can't do this ... I won't do this. It was discipline that had gotten her to this point in her life. It was discipline that might save her.

She found the courage to sidestep away from him. She remembered who she was today. Not who she'd been with Blake. She was not that person anymore.

She spoke carefully, first looking down and then looking him right in the eyes.

"I'm a different person now, Blake. I'm not right for you. You're not right for me."

He shook his head "no" and placed both of his hands on her shoulders. "Honey, I need to help you jog your memory. We were good together. We had fun together. Give me another chance." He smiled sweetly. She knew his volatile emotions could change in an instant—from loving to dangerous.

She needed some distance. He was too close. She put her hands on his massive chest and gently pushed him back. She didn't want to risk being close if his rage flared.

She steadied her voice. "Blake, Honey, no. I loved you once. We did have good times ... but that was a long time ago. I've changed. I've created a new life for myself. I have friends, a job."

She stood tall and waited. She was all alone with him.

"Sorry to hear that." His voice was low, dead. She

watched as his eyes went from warm with desire to dull, cold black stone. He pulled himself up tall. He put his hands together and cracked his knuckles. She knew he felt she was his property. Running away from him had been a blow to his ego—one he would never forget. She would have to pay the price.

He moved closer. She fingered the panic button on her remote, ready if she needed to . . . but who would hear? She didn't want him any closer. What should she do? If she ran, he might shoot. If he got ahold of her, he could drag her off and rape her. He could beat her senseless in the parking lot and leave without a trace. Seconds seemed like hours.

She would try one more approach. "Blake, Honey—"

Before she could say another word, she heard voices in the parking lot. Nick and Nancy were walking out to their car. They were laughing and talking. She could hear bits and pieces of their conversation.

Where were they parked? Would they see her? Did she dare?

She had to make a move.

"Nick, Nancy! How are you guys, did you have fun?" she yelled out.

"Staci?" Nancy responded.

"Over here!"

Blake backed off. He glared at her, his eyes burning with rage. The veins in his neck bulged purple. His body went rigid, and he clenched and unclenched his hands into fists. She knew he could kill her. She had seen this before. He had beaten her, she had come back, and he had beaten her again.

Blake's presence meant her past and present worlds had collided. Someone who knew her dark and dirty secrets now walked in her pristine present. An overpowering sadness nearly brought her to tears. Was everything over?

Nick and Nancy approached. They saw the hulk of a man standing over Staci.

"Car trouble, Staci?" Nick asked.

She knew Nick was streetwise, could smell danger and was on alert.

"Yes. This man was going to help me, but now that you're here . . ."

"Happy to help . . . anytime, Ma'am." Blake backed off. "You're lucky to have friends," he said. He put his hat on his head and walked away to a dark pickup parked close to the bar.

They all watched as he got in and drove off in a cloud of dust.

"What was that all about?" Nick asked.

Staci hesitated. She inhaled sharply and decided to tell one version of the truth.

"He's someone I knew . . . a long time ago. He happened to be in the bar. He hoped I was still interested."

"And you're not . . . I take it?" Nancy replied. "He looked pretty pissed off to me. I've seen angry rejected men. Guys like that can hurt a girl."

"Yes, they can," Staci replied soberly. They all looked in the direction of the truck now long gone.

Staci needed to change the subject. "Come on, guys, let's go home! I hope you had a great time. We had a great time. We love you both!" She smiled, trying to hold herself together for a few more minutes.

"We love you too, Staci," Nancy replied and hugged her. "Be careful out there, girl."

"Yeah, Staci, be careful. You shouldn't be out in a parking lot this late at night alone," Nick said.

"I know . . . I know better . . . thanks, guys. Travel safe."

Staci walked to her car, got in and locked the doors. She started to shake. The demons of her past had finally caught her. Overcome by a wave of grief propelled by the loss of hope, tears filled her eyes, and she rested her head on the steering wheel and sobbed with loneliness and sadness. Her venture into a joyful and meaningful life had been so fleeting. She had risked everything for a glimpse of the world that so many people around her seemed to have and take for granted, but it was not hers to live. Within minutes, her emotions had taken a roller-coaster ride from happiness to sheer terror to depression.

Exhausted, she started to drive, feeling utterly alone and adrift in the world. She wondered how he had found her and what she should do. Her lie would be exposed. She was not only vulnerable but threatened now, without protection. Tears blurred her vision. Disoriented, she drove slowly and carefully through the darkness.

Suddenly she was freezing cold. The icepick of fear slashed through her, taking her breath away. Heart pounding, she sucked in deep breaths to find her steady center. Her hands were wet with sweat, and she hung on tight to the steering wheel. The primal instinct for survival took charge. The need to live pulled her out of her tailspin into sadness. Adrenaline coursed through her body, putting her on high alert. She was fully aware of her priorities. *What will he do next?*

She couldn't wait to find out the answer. She knew what she had to do.

SANTOS

Overnight, the weather turned miserable. Five inches of torrential rain fell in under eight hours. Street flooding closed roads and submerged the cars that dared risk the rushing water. Twenty thousand homes lost electricity. Thankfully, Santos had spent the night at Camilla's. The power had stayed on all night. Camilla's guest room was quickly becoming Santos's room. She was enjoying the time with her sister and sharing her adventures in love and work.

Though it had been a late night at Mother's, Santos was happy in the morning as she braved the crazy Houston drivers who drove as if they had never seen rain. The night had been an incredible success—so many surprises. They'd had so much fun!

When she walked through the double doors of the CCU, she was looking forward to seeing everyone, reminiscing about the evening. There was no one in the lounge when she tucked her purse in her locker. That was unusual. Santos headed to the conference room for morning report. The door was closed. She wondered what was going on. When she opened the door, she found it full of staff, both night shift and day. Everyone looked up. Kathleen's face was red, and she was crying. Why was she still here? Staci had her arm around the young nurse.

"Oh, Santos, I'm so glad you're here. We had a terrible night. Mr. Hope-Simon died!"

Santos sat down next to Kathleen, her heart sinking. "Oh, no—what happened?"

"I was just telling everyone. He seemed just fine early

in the evening. We talked about his going home on Monday . . . how he was at peace . . . how his children were coming in for a visit, maybe their last visit. He wanted to see them while he could still carry on a conversation, enjoy their time together, share a meal . . ." She started to sob.

"It's okay, let it out," Staci said. She looked over Kathleen's head at Santos. Her eyes were sad, and they glistened with tears.

Kathleen blew her nose, took the water Staci offered, and continued. "I walked into his room at about nine o'clock, and he was unresponsive. I tried to wake him, but I couldn't. I shook him and he didn't move. He still had his morphine drip, so I disconnected it and ran just fluids. He had bradycardia, but his heart was still regular. I shook him again, and all of a sudden, he flat lined. The monitor alarm went off, and everybody came running."

She started crying again. "There was nothing we could do! He had a DNR . . . and I know he was ready, but his family—his family was so devastated. I didn't know what to say to them. Mrs. Hope-Simon got down on her knees by his bed and sobbed. They didn't get a chance to say good-bye. I feel like I really screwed up. Like it was my fault."

The door to the conference room opened, and Sandra walked in. "What's going on?" Her voice was cold. She tapped her pen on the ever-present notebook and arched her eyebrows, questioning. Santos thought she sounded more Gestapo-like than ever.

Staci explained the best she could. Sandra appeared bored with the narrative.

"Kathleen, we can talk about this after morning report," Sandra said. Her voice was firm as if to say, "Get a grip, girl."

The interim director looked at the group who had assembled for rounds. "I think we need to reexamine this Pathways program. Something is not working. Maybe we're spending too much time planning and not enough time on patient care?" She cocked her head to the side and waited for a response, but none came. "I'll be in my office when you're ready to see me, Kathleen." She walked out the door.

Kathleen looked at Santos with fearful eyes. "I can't face her right now. She'll tear me to shreds. I'm already a puddle . . . a mess."

"We'll take care of it," Staci replied.

"Don't worry, Kathleen—you need to go home. She'll be ticked off that you didn't follow orders, but I'll take the heat," Santos said. "I'll tell her you were sick and I sent you home."

They made it through rounds. The high of last night, the joy of the evening together had faded, already a distant memory. Had it really happened? Sometime, they would have to go through all of the pictures and the videos they'd taken. Sometime—away from work—they could relive the night.

"Hey, do you have a minute?" Staci called to Santos as she started to leave the conference room. "I know we've got to get to work, but there's something I need to say."

Santos turned around. Staci looked exhausted. She had blue smudges under her eyes, and her usual perfect posture was gone. Preoccupied with the trauma over Mr. Hope-Simon's death, Santos hadn't noticed.

"Sure, what's wrong?"

Staci moved close to Santos. "I just wanted to say thank you—for all you've done for me. For welcoming me into this unit, into your life."

Such a lovely thing to say, but why now? Santos reached

out to grasp Staci's hands. They were ice cold. She squeezed them and looked into her eyes. Staci dodged her look. Santos hoped that her words would bring her around. "I was glad to—though not at first. You won me over."

Staci met her eyes. "You're a great teacher, a wonderful role model. You're the best friend I've ever had." Staci's eyes started to fill with tears.

"Staci, what's wrong?" Santos asked and pulled her to an alcove in the hallway in search of a more private location.

"Nothing that I can talk about—something personal—I can't talk about it now . . . Well, I can, just a little." Staci paused to take a breath. "Blake showed up last night. Remember the guy I told you about who was a walking nightmare? He found me at Mother's, in the parking lot. He wants me back. No one leaves Blake until he decides. Thank God Nick and Nancy came out when they did. I told him that I've moved on, have another life. He didn't like it." Staci paused to take a deep breath. "I don't know what he's going to do next. I'm scared to death—if he finds me alone, what he'll do."

Santos's smile faded, and she considered what to do. "Do you need a place to stay? Do you feel safe?"

"He doesn't know where I live. I don't think he does, but I'm not sure. I'm just going to have to be really, really careful."

"Let me know . . . you can always move in with me." Santos hesitated, thinking about last year. She didn't want to attract more trouble home or bring it to Camilla's or one of her sisters. Perhaps one of her brothers would stay with them—at least for a while. Staci needed shelter. "I don't have a lot of space, but you would be further away from the Medical Center. Just let me know. We'll work it out somehow."

"Thank you, Santos. I appreciate your offer. Don't

think I need it right now."

"Okay. It's an open offer, anytime." Santos smiled. "We've got to get back to work."

"Oh, Santos." Staci reached out to grasp Santos's arm, holding her back. "I just want you to know how grateful I am for what you've done for me—more than you can ever imagine. You've shown me that there is another way to live—to love. You've given me a glimpse into a life that is meaningful. You need to know that . . . thank you. I love you, Santos."

Santos reached out and hugged Staci. Staci held on to her almost as if she was—seeing her for the last time? Staci felt fragile, vulnerable—like she would break into pieces. Worry clouded Santos's thoughts. This was unusual. Staci was always so driven and tough.

"I love you too," the words spilled out of Santos. Over the past weeks, she had quickly bonded with Staci, but she could sense there was more to the story—and Staci wasn't telling.

"And you had better marry that man—soon! Time's a wastin', girl!" Staci smiled for the first time that morning. "You're meant for each other."

"Circling back," Santos began seriously, "remember, I'm off after today for two shifts. I'll be back for your shift before you go off for a few days. If you need me while I'm off, call me on my cell."

"Will do. Got anything special planned?" Staci asked.

"Time to get to work, Partner."

Staci smiled and deflected Santos's attempt to change the subject. "You hear me now? About marrying that man?"

"I hear you," Santos replied. They walked out together, and Santos added another worry to her growing list. *What else is going on here?*

PATRICK

"Happiness is somebody to love,
Something to do,
And something to hope for."
Chinese Proverb

"I feel like we're playing hooky," Santos said as she looked out the window of Patrick's jeep. The Texas Hill Country, in its prime, was rushing by. The sun was shining, with not a cloud in the light blue sky. The grass was lush and green, the woods were dotted with white blossoms, and Carolina jasmine's flowering yellow vines hugged trees and telephone poles. Birds' nests hid behind the foliage while parents fiercely protected their progeny.

"We're not playing hooky. We have the next two days off," Patrick replied. He looked over at her and smiled. She cocked her head and smiled, dazzling him. Her russet hair was captured in a lose ponytail tied with a red ribbon. He was happy and at peace. They were going away together for the first time. The trip was their secret, a private getaway. Though the trip would be expensive, this was their first night together, and he wanted to make it special. Work was taking its toll on both of them. They needed to get away, focus on each other, and celebrate life.

"So—tell me again. How did you find out about this place?"

"I've actually known about it for a while. But Richard told me he took Julie there for her fiftieth birthday. It's a special place. Midweek, it should be really quiet."

"It sounds great. I read about it online." Santos sat back and breathed deeply. "I really need this, Patrick. I need to get out of town, get away from work. I need perspective. I'm off balance. I love our patients and the team. It's devastating when our patients don't make it. I suppose I should develop a thicker skin and put up more boundaries, but then, I don't think I would be as good a nurse. Emma and Heather are a huge loss. Sandra is, well, something else. I know that evil walks the earth, but I've never met someone as dangerous as she is . . . and she's in a power position as a manager. My gut tells me to stay as far away from her as possible."

"I'm with you, 100 percent," Patrick replied. Then he smiled at her. "Let's look forward—not back."

"Every mile we drive is a mile away from our troubles—right?" Santos replied and smiled back. He loved that smile with all his heart.

"Right. Time to have some fun—alone."

They were heading to the Inn at Dos Brisas in the Chappell Hill area. Set on a ranch of over three hundred rolling acres, the small Relais & Chateau property was composed of beautiful casitas, haciendas, a stable, and a main lodge with a bar and a *Forbes* five-star restaurant. Each room had a fireplace, a small kitchen, and an outdoor patio. The restaurant was farm-to-table, relying heavily on locally grown produce.

He wondered about Santos's expectations about the weekend and if she would be happy with his plans. He had worked hard to arrange all the details in such a way that they could both just relax and be together.

"So what are we going to do when we get there?"

"Well, we'll check in, look around. Pick up our golf cart."

"Golf cart?"

"Yes, each casita has a golf cart to get around the property."

"Fun!"

"We have dinner reservations for later tonight. I think we should try the chef's tasting and maybe split a wine pairing—so it's not too much wine. Breakfast is in the casita in the morning, whenever we want it."

"Sounds perfect. What about lunch?"

"Well, I have a little surprise for you for lunch." Patrick looked over at Santos and smiled. It had been fun to plan the special romantic meal. He hoped it would work out as well as the staff promised him it would.

"Oh, come on—tell me."

"Then it won't be a surprise." He smiled and returned his eyes to the winding road. "Why don't you tell me what you think about the book?"

He had given Santos a book, *The Three Marriages*, by the bestselling author, poet, and speaker David Whyte. Patrick had first seen David at a national conference and was not only impressed, but inspired and deeply touched by his wisdom and writing. The book was about life's three marriages: work, relationships, and the inner self. Whyte asked the reader to reconsider the concept of life balance and think about these important commitments as conversing with and actually inspiring the other.

He saw that Santos had brought the book along, flagging numerous areas.

"Okay, I'm not finished with it yet . . . it takes a while to digest. What he says, and what the other authors and poets say, really makes you stop and think. It's right on with where I think we are in our lives—at a crossroads of commitment. I loved the poetry and how he drew from other poets and authors as well as included his own work."

She opened the book to a flag. "This part really spoke to me: 'To glimpse our vocation, we must learn how to be sought out and found by a work as much as we strive to identify it ourselves. We must make ourselves findable by being seen; to do that, we must hazard ourselves.' I really like how he uses the word *hazard*. It's so much more powerful than just saying, 'make yourself vulnerable.' And I like how he describes the belief that we must fall in love with our work."

Patrick listened closely, drinking in her every word, enjoying her voice, her nearness. Santos continued, "It reminds me of the book *Flow,* though it's different. *Flow* says that optimal life experiences don't just happen. They require work to achieve. Csikszentmihalyi believes that optimal life experiences occur when we *stretch* our minds and bodies to do something difficult and worthwhile. It's when we take a challenge and reach for it that we expand ourselves."

"Did you experience 'flow' when you and the team put on the musical show for Nick and Nancy? It seems like music and theater would be logical and incredible places to experience it."

"That's right. We're talking about that in the music portion of Pathways. But just think about how it feels when we all work together to save a life. There's such exhilaration when we work as hard as we can, use all of our talents and skills, and work as a team. It's so joyful."

"It is . . . and exhausting. It takes everything from us. But when we look back, there are wonderful feelings of accomplishment," Patrick agreed. "The great thing about health care is we use every talent, every skill; we draw from every life experience and every fiber of our being to help, to intervene to improve health and save lives."

"And support them when they need to die," Santos added. She was quiet for a moment. He wondered if she was thinking of the patients who had so recently passed away. "So what David Whyte has to say is that if we want to evolve, be the best that we can be, we must also invest in ourselves and in our relationships. Just focusing on the work will not replenish the self, feed the spirit, or restore us."

Patrick replied, "I think that David, and this is only my interpretation, believes that the three marriages are sort of like a three-legged stool—they support each other and make a person whole. If we don't attend to our own health, our inner development, our spiritual energy, we can't give at work or in a marriage. I believe the presence of all of these strengthens us as an individual."

"Synergistically—we become better because of the interplay?"

"Yes. I think we have the opportunity to learn from all of the relationships we have and grow from them, as long as they are healthy."

"And stay away from emotional vampires like Sandra—preferably never have one as your boss," Santos added.

"Yeah." Patrick nodded, and his thoughts turned to their current dilemma. He rarely felt powerless—this was an exception. He needed to work this through. Perhaps a talk with Richard was in order. Patrick believed that true leaders didn't accept the status quo, particularly when it was bad. They were all about creating healthy environments. Right now the unit was as sick as any of their patients.

"Well, this time is about us. Sorry I brought her up."

"That's okay. She's a part of our work challenge right now, unfortunately." He felt anger rise up inside as he thought of how Sandra had affected the people he cared about and the work he so passionately believed in. "She makes it more difficult to do what we need to do—and she takes energy from us that really should go to our patients and our other teammates."

"I really miss Heather—and Emma. Though work has always been hard, they made it easy compared to Sandra."

The talk with Santos was solidifying his intentions of what he needed to do when they returned to work. "I think that's another point—we've talked forever about how important your boss is, but David's point brings front and center how the energy of good intentions and focus on the same goal make work easier."

"And caring for each other," Santos said. "Emma and Heather care about us. We care about them. It really makes a difference. I'd do anything for either of them. Our team has great energy. We're so good together. Even on stage!" She smiled, remembering. "That was so much fun. You're right. That was flow. I think Staci missed her calling."

She fell silent for a moment. Patrick cast a glance at her and saw that she was frowning. "Speaking of Staci—I think there's something going on with her—beyond Blake catching up with her. That's scary enough, but I have a feeling there's more."

Patrick spotted the sign for the inn and made a left onto a narrow gravel road. The property, surrounded by a white fence, had a gated entrance.

"We're here?"

"Looks like it."

"I'm excited," Santos said. "A little nervous, too." She looked down at the book in her lap.

Patrick brought the car to a stop, put it in park, and turned to her. Where had she said they were? *A crossroads of commitment.* "We don't have to do anything you don't want to do. If we end up just falling asleep together tonight ... that's enough for me. All I want, more than anything, is to fall asleep with you and wake up with you in my arms."

Santos leaned over and kissed him warmly. Her dark eyes were shining.

"Thank you, Patrick. You're the best."

"Ready now?"

"Yes." She gave him a big smile.

His heart moved. *She's so beautiful. Will she be mine? Will I be able to wake up with her every morning of my life?*

Patrick drove up to the gate and parked close to the speaker on the security panel. He pressed the button and gave his name, and the gate slowly opened.

They checked in and took a quick tour of the main building, which included a lounge, bar, dining room, and outdoor swimming pool. Huge, well-manicured gardens flanked the main lodge. The herb garden overflowed with rosemary, basil, thyme, mint, oregano, and lavender. Patrick watched as Santos reached down to touch and smell the herbs. The roses were fragrant and glorious in their prime.

A member of the staff guided them to one of the casitas with a view of the hills. It was so quiet they could hear the wind rustle the leaves of the trees. Butterflies danced on the colorful flaming orange flowers of a bush. A cardinal and its mate chirped from the branches of an olive tree. Green and blue sparkling dragonflies, big as small drones, swooped up and around.

"This soothes my soul," Santos said as Patrick unlocked the door of the casita.

They walked into the cool, large room, tiled with terracotta. The vaulted casita was furnished in a comfortable ranch style. The large bed was covered with an antique quilt, and a stone fireplace with a small seating area completed the room. Walls of windows brought the beauty of the outside into the room.

"This is gorgeous," Santos said. She put down her overnight bag and purse and started to explore. "Look, we have snacks in the refrigerator. There's coffee for the morning. Looks like we could sleep with the windows open. Oh, look at the patio! Can we have breakfast here? I wonder if it's too warm to have a fire tonight."

"You aren't excited, are you?" Patrick laughed at her nonstop commentary.

Her eyes shone in his direction. His heart thrilled at her happiness.

"Yes, I am excited. Should we unpack or eat?"

"Whatever you want."

"I'm hungry," she said quietly. "Actually, I'm starving, Patrick."

"Well, and as we know from experience, we don't want that to continue."

"I won't get cranky, Patrick, not here." She looked up at him and smiled.

"Well, let's get going. Lunch is the surprise."

"Where are we going?"

Patrick opened the door of the casita and waved Santos out. He headed to the golf cart. "Hop in. They told me to drive down the road until I cross the bridge. Take a left at the creek and we should see the table in the woods."

"A picnic? Oh, that sounds wonderful! Such a beautiful day. This is so much fun!"

Patrick was relieved and at the same time thrilled that she was so pleased with his choices. He realized that she enjoyed the same kind of things that he did. He could ramp down his anxiety about making her happy. She was the far-thest thing from some of the drama queens who had crossed his path. If you did not pamper them, they pouted. They needed to be the center of the world. Santos, by con-trast, rarely indulged herself. She was all about others and took joy in small and everyday experiences. He was starting to let go and enjoy the moment. Planning was over. It was now up to each of them to create the experience.

He drove the golf cart down the gravel road and made the turn by the creek.

"Do you see it?" Santos asked. They both looked through the trees. "There! There it is!"

He spotted a table covered with a red-checked table-cloth and drove through the wooded path that led up to it. They got out of the golf cart and walked down a narrow path through the woods. A feast awaited them. The food's presentation was unlike any picnic Patrick had ever seen. It looked like a photo shoot for *Food & Wine* or something fit for visiting royalty. Each dish was presented in a small or large metal box, a little bigger than a bento box. Santos gig-gled like a little girl as she opened tin after tin filled with one treasure after another. There was fried chicken, still warm and crispy; mixed-green salad with assorted home-made dressings; cheeses with fresh, crunchy French baguettes; potato salad on ice.

"Oh, you missed this," Patrick said, peeking into one of the tins. "Close your eyes and smell."

Santos rolled her eyes but did what he said. "Oh my goodness, chocolate-chip cookies!"

"My favorite," he said. "I think I need to try one now." He picked one up and took a bite. "They're still warm. Have a bite."

Santos took a bite of the chewy, crunchy goodness and said, "I'm in food heaven."

More pleased than he could say, Patrick dug into the picnic basket and pulled out white china dinner plates, silverware, and red-checkered cloth napkins. There were bottles of ice-cold water and a chilled half-bottle of wine and two wineglasses.

"What a feast," Santos said. "I need to take a picture before we get started."

They took a variety of pictures with her phone and settled into lunch.

"Would you like some wine? It's just a glass apiece," Patrick asked.

"Why not? We're splurging here. We're not driving—except the golf cart!"

He laughed at how she had completely lost herself in the afternoon. Her spirit was lighter and more fun than he had ever seen.

They spent hours working their way through the fabulous food, enjoying the tranquility of the setting, the warmth of the sun, and the breezes that kept the insects at bay. They kissed between courses and talked about family, life, and their hopes and dreams. They took time to share their mutual views of marriage and commitment. Then talked with concern about the many people they knew who were divorced. They shared their views of why a marriage might fail. Patrick felt that this moment in time—where they were truly alone and had time to talk—took their relationship to another level of understanding that felt peaceful and right. They couldn't always escape the worries and troubles of life, but they could find places where a planned oasis could give them rest. Most of all, he wanted to build happy memories.

"Patrick, I think I need a nap after this," Santos said reluctantly, "or I'll fall asleep in my soup tonight. And I brought a special dress to wear. I want to be able to stay awake through dinner." She looked at him, her dark eyes sparkling with love and happiness. He wanted her so much. Not just for a day; for the rest of his life. She was the love of his life. He took her in his arms and kissed her deeply. The kiss jolted him. He wanted more.

"I never want this day to end," she said. "I've never been this happy. Thank you, Patrick. This is such a wonderful escape—such a good thing for us. We are making more memories." She smiled.

He couldn't stop himself from expressing what he felt. "Santos, I love you so much. I want to give you everything. I want to be with you, forever."

She smiled and hugged him. Then she tilted her head up and looked in his eyes. "I love you too, Patrick. Kiss me."

He wanted to drown in her kisses—consume her and be one with her. He would never have enough of her sweet, soft lips. He wanted to lose himself, not only in this moment, but in her arms. Did she want the same?

They came up for air. Santos smiled. She reached up and traced her finger across his lips. He shuddered with pleasure. Her warm chocolate eyes were dark with longing.

"Let's go take that nap," she said. His heart beat faster. He needed no further encouragement. He found his balance, stood up, and pulled her to her feet. She looked up at him. Suddenly, he surprised himself when he leaned over, picked her up and carried her to the golf cart. She laughed all along the way. "Don't drop me!"

"I've carried you before, you just don't remember," he said laughing. "This is a lot more fun."

He put her in the golf cart and walked over to his side.

He smiled, happy, as he watched her take one last look at their picnic table full of empty boxes, and he caught her smile.

STACI

"When I despair, I remember that all through history
the way of truth and love have always won.
There have been tyrants and murderers, and for a time,
they can seem invincible, but in the end, they always fall.
Think of it—always."

Mahatma Gandhi

Staci knew what she had to do. She had no choice. She had to go away. Leave everything that was important. Leave this life, her work, and the team. Yet it was the last thing she wanted to do.

The one thing she would take with her, the most valuable intangible, was the woman she had become. She had learned so much, about people and life, and by learning she had evolved. Santos had told her once, "When someone really learns something, they change their behavior. You can teach people many things—about the dangers of smoking or avoiding certain foods that trigger atrial fib—but until they really learn, really internalize something, they will never change. And learning can be painful. Until someone has a heart attack—it's like a wakeup call or a whack on the side of the head—they may not change their workaholic style, their eating habits, or lose weight. They have to learn to be different."

Staci was not the same woman who had begun this charade. She had received a gift—insight into a reality she had never dreamed possible, where relationships bloomed, people cared about each other, and hard work produced important results. She was stronger, but paradoxically, this maturation had come with a deep sense of humility. She felt unworthy to be a part of this world. She had not earned her place. She had conned and manipulated her way in. And she knew she had to leave.

The illusion of reality she had created was fragile, and it was falling apart. Blake's rage made it clear that her life was in danger. Survival meant running, going underground.

But how? When?

She had not seen or heard from him since the incident in the parking lot. Maybe he'd made another conquest? Found someone else? *Wishful thinking.* It was only a matter of time before he tracked her down again. Sam had called Staci again and told her that Blake had been in touch. *Damn Sam for telling him about me in the first place. Stupid me for talking to Sam.* She cut off all communication with Sam then and there—too dangerous.

Though conflicted, for this last little while before she found the opportunity to run, she could still find solace in work. She could make a difference working, helping the team and her patients. She loved coaching the new graduates, giving them emotional support and words of wisdom. They seemed so young—though they were very close to her age. She had already lived a longer, more painful life than most of them would ever experience or understand. It was easy to stay in character as a nurse, to play the part. It was a part she loved.

While she was busy, she could push Blake out of her thoughts. Sleep was another matter. He emerged in her dreams, chasing her, getting closer and closer. She would wake in a cold sweat, the sheets tangled around her legs, her heart threatening to explode in her chest.

Her humility created a building awareness that she was dangerous to patients. She was walking on eggshells. She could make a mistake or be caught at any time. Blake's showing up was a warning. Her time was running out—precious time in a brief life that had been rich and rewarding. She knew it was best to get ahead of discovery. And who knew when Mary Stevens's body would show up? This new life had always been risky. Now it was dangerous.

She longed to talk with Santos about her dilemma. The burden she carried was staggering. It darkened her every day. But telling Santos might implicate her, and Staci would protect her friend at all cost.

She had not seen Santos in a couple of days, but Patrick was back at work today. Staci decided to work the remaining two shifts in the pay period. She had avoided setting up a bank account, opting instead for a Bluebird cash card with automatic deposits. Disciplined about saving money, she had a large stash of cash. She had already started packing up her meager possessions—the cherished suede vest, the sheet music from practice, and the book of photos Nick and Nancy had made for each of them. These treasures would always remind her of the happy times. She would take the textbooks to Half Price Books, leave the journals somewhere. She would ditch her throwaway phone, buy a new one, and cut off all communication with her past. Talking to Sam had been stupid. Her heart broke realizing she could never talk to Santos again. It would be too dangerous—for both of them for different reasons.

Her mind worked in overdrive thinking through the details while juggling the complexity of work. She walked across the CCU to check on one of her patients.

As she approached Gelena Scalina's cubicle, she noticed the curtains drawn around the bed. *I left the cubicle curtains open. Did she want to try and sleep?*

Staci quietly entered the cubicle and scanned the area. What she saw stopped her short.

Mrs. Scalina's head was to the side, her eyes closed. The monitor quietly beeped NSR. Sandra was standing next to the bed, her back to Staci. Staci watched as Sandra took the IV tubing, found a port on one of the lines, picked up a loaded syringe from the bed, and uncapped the needle.

"What are you doing?" Her voice was assertive. Her gut warned of life-threatening danger to her vulnerable patient. Protective anger flared, compounded by her disdain for Sandra. "You don't need to be here."

Sandra ignored Staci for a moment, preparing to give the medication IV push. "Oh, I answered her call button. She wanted something for pain." Sandra responded calmly. Her eyes never left the IV tubing and syringe. All Staci's instincts told her the woman was covering for something.

"I don't think so. I just gave her something for pain— a few minutes ago." Staci moved toward Sandra and the syringe and held out her hand. "Give me that!"

Sandra hesitated at first and then emptied the contents of the syringe in the wastebasket. Staci was putting the pieces together—sudden deaths, the toxic leader, success at any cost. "We can have this analyzed . . . we *will* have this analyzed."

Sandra looked at her. Her lips curled into a smug smile, and her eyes were cold gray steel. "We need to talk." She thought for a second. "Not here. Come with me."

Staci picked up the wastebasket, reconsidered, and put it down again. She followed Sandra out of the cubicle. "I'm not going to your office. We stay out in the open."

Sandra walked with confidence, shoulders erect, to the stairwell door. She opened it and said, "Out in the open enough for you?" She walked through the door.

Staci looked around. No one was in sight. No help on the horizon. She had no choice, so she reluctantly followed.

The stairwell door closed behind them.

"What were you doing?" Staci demanded.

"Just helping her along a little—no use in wasting any more of our time and resources. She was ready to die. She was on the Pathway list."

The callous comment infuriated Staci. "She was on the list because she wanted to die at home—not in a cold hospital bed, all alone. We don't have the right to end someone's life . . . before they have time to say good-bye . . . anytime—we don't have the right!" Staci's raised her voice in outrage.

Sandra tapped her foot on the concrete, apparently bored with the conversation. The tapping echoed in the silent stairwell. Staci felt dismissed, diminished—invisible. Sandra always had that effect on her. She got ready for round two of the debate when all of a sudden, her brain leaped into action and she began to fill in the pieces of the puzzle. Two patients on the Pathway had died, right before their transfer out of the unit.

"Mrs. Cartwright and Mr. Hope-Simon—both died unexpectedly. They were both Pathway patients. Did *you* kill them? What about Mr. McIntire?"

"Moi?" Sandra said innocently. "I didn't kill them, I just helped them along. It was painless and quick. They were ready to die . . . so what? What I used is impossible to trace. No one will ever know."

"You bitch!"

"Your interpretation. Some might call me an angel of mercy."

"You have no mercy. You have no *conscience*. You don't

have an ounce of compassion. I would call you an angel of death." Staci was shaking with anger. "You deserve to be punished. I'm going to turn you in."

"Staci, let's be realistic. Who are they going to believe? You or me?" Sandra cocked her head to the side, smiling. "You're a traveler, I'm management. I've got Whiting eating out of the palm of my hand. Elaine is thrilled with my work—especially the increase in unit efficiency. No one will believe you. You're a nothing."

The sucker punch hit Staci hard—because it was true.

"They *will* believe me," she insisted, against her own fears, against the condemnation in her heart. "I've got evidence against you—a wastebasket full of evidence and a patient who could potentially ID you."

"Now, now, Staci—we're both big girls here. I've got a proposition for you." Sandra smiled confidently. "I'll trade you—a secret for a secret."

"No way," Staci replied. "You're going to jail."

"I don't think so." Sandra shook her head. "*You're* the one who is going to jail."

"Oh, yeah?" Staci kept her cool. She stood eye to eye with Sandra. She was livid now, and her anger was galvanizing. She held her ground and moved closer. They were within inches of each other on the edge of the stairs.

"You aren't who you say you are. I was suspicious about you from the beginning—so I began my own private search. I've never seen your resume because you don't have one. You're not from Mars, Iowa—no, you're an impostor. You aren't Mary S. Stevens who goes by 'Staci.' You took her identify, pretended to be a nurse. You've committed a felony. You're facing criminal charges. And maybe there are other dirty little secrets in your past that will be uncovered during the investigation. Like *how* you obtained her identity? As soon as we end this conversation, I'm calling security—then heading right up to Elaine's office." Sandra's face turned red, ugly with rage as the ice princess's cool façade cracked. She spit out, "You're going to jail! Who's calling who a bitch?"

The spew of venomous, devastating words stung Staci speechless. Her worst fear had come to pass. This ruthless monster would stop at nothing to take her down. There was no escape now. Her life was over, ended before she could run. Her eyes started to fill with tears. "Can't we talk about this?" Staci pleaded. "Please let me explain."

She reached out, and Sandra put out her hand out in a "stop" gesture, then stepped back to move away from Staci. She underestimated how close she was to the stairs. As Staci watched in horror, Sandra teetered on the edge in her heels, then lost her balance. She grabbed for the railing but missed. Staci reached for her—too late. Sandra fell. Her hands flew into the air, and her mouth opened in a silent scream. Her back hit the stairs first, and her head slammed back in a whiplash against the edge of the concrete. Her body went limp and rolled to the landing.

Staci heard Sandra wheeze and gasp for air. Then there was silence.

Staci ran down the stairs. Sandra's eyes were wide open, her legs splayed, her right arm thrown over her head. She did not move. Staci felt for a carotid pulse—thready, then nothing. Blood was pooling on the concrete. Her neck was obviously broken, the back of her head crushed from the fall. Staci's mind rushed back to another woman, another death. That woman had been innocent. That had woman opened the door to this life. Sandra had closed it.

Staci's first impulse was panic. Over the pounding of her heart, she listened . . . the stairwell was completely silent.

There was no one coming up the stairs or opening the door from the unit. She took a few deep breaths to calm herself and then looked around the stairwell. *No cameras.* She would be safe if she could get out of there without discovery. It had been an accident. But it would be difficult to explain, and she couldn't risk the police looking into her background. There was nothing she could do. Sandra was dead.

She ran back up the stairs to the CCU. She opened the door to the unit and looked around. Everyone was busy with patients. She walked calmly over to Mrs. Scalina's bed, her mind racing. *When will they discover the body? How do I tell them who was killing our patients? Will they think it was me?*

She opened the cubicle curtain. The monitor read NSR. She walked over to see her patient more closely. Her breathing was rapid but not distressed. A piece of hair had fallen across her face, and Staci gently tucked it back. Sandra hadn't had time to inject the drug.

"Staci, when can I go home?" Mrs. Scalina mumbled. "I can never get any sleep here. I want to spend my last days . . . or hours . . . with my family. I miss my cat Phoebe. I want to sleep with her on my chest again. Phoebe always knows how I feel, when I'm sick, when to come to me . . . she's better than any dog I've known, more loving and tender. She's a healer and the most intuitive pet I've ever known. She's more sensitive than most people."

Staci let out an audible sigh of relief. Her patient was okay.

"Phoebe must be an old soul, then. She needs you and you need her." Staci took Mrs. Scalina's small, dry hand in hers and rubbed it warm.

"I think she loves me too. She's an Abyssinian. It's one

of the oldest breeds—thought to be the most intelligent. It's like she has ESP. Abyssinians are people pets. I wish you could meet her."

Staci tried to focus on her patient, but her attention was wandering as her heart raced. She was still in shock and preoccupied with the death in the stairwell. *Got to focus. Be present. One thing at a time.*

"I'll check in with the Pathway team, but I'm pretty sure we can get you home tomorrow. We'll be transferring you in an ambulance. When your family comes in today, I'll ask them to bring you a clean nightgown, robe, and slippers."

"Oh, Honey . . . that would make me so happy." Mrs. Scalina smiled and promptly dozed off. She was sleeping more and more these days.

Staci watched her for a moment, checked all of the lines and pumps—all of which would likely go when she went home. Everything looked okay.

"Code Blue!—CCU stairwell!" someone shouted. "Call a Code Blue!"

Staci looked in the direction of the shouts. The stairwell was quickly swarming with white coats and green scrubs. Staci purposefully walked to the scene with trepidation. Richard Whiting picked his way through the throng and made it to the stairwell landing where Sandra lay. He got down on one knee to take a closer look. Seconds passed.

"Everybody out, please. I'm afraid she's gone. Patrick, stay with me." He looked up the stairs, and his eyes fixed on Staci. "Staci, can you come here please?"

Staci went cold with dread. Her heart was beating so fast she could hardly breathe.

The stairwell finally emptied of white coats and green scrubs. It was quiet.

"What do you think happened here?" Richard said to Patrick.

Patrick responded quickly. "Looks like she fell—do we need to do something to investigate?"

"Could it be as simple as that?" Richard stood up and looked around. "No cameras that I can see . . . but I'll check in with security and see if anything caught her entering the stairwell. I also need to check in with legal to see if we're required to launch an investigation or if we need to get the police involved."

Staci felt faint. She closed her eyes for a moment, hoping the men would take her reaction as grief or shock over Sandra's death and nothing more.

Patrick said, "This isn't my area, but Dad was a prosecuting attorney. They would look for evidence of foul play." He paused, obviously thinking about what to say next. "Richard, this may not be the time, but she was bad news. She wasn't the manager she pretended to be. She was bullying the new grads. She micromanaged us, demeaned us. She was not the kind of leader we need here. She wasn't Heather, or Emma. Now is not the time to get into the details and give you all of the examples. Bottom line—she was one of the most toxic people I have ever met. "

Staci wanted to cheer.

"Patrick, I'm really surprised to hear this. But what are you saying? Are you thinking someone might have pushed her? Were the staff that upset?"

Staci panicked and willed herself to calm down as Patrick answered. "No, I'm not saying that anyone on our team would ever do this. Sandra's style was mean. It was abusive and demoralizing. But I can't imagine that any one of us would do this. I just . . . it wouldn't surprise me if she had other enemies."

Richard looked down at Sandra's body and shook his head. Then he looked up at Patrick, his face creased with concern. "No one has talked to me about any of this. I heard a few things, but I didn't think they were serious. I thought they were just people reacting to change. I know how everyone loves and misses Heather."

Richard paused and raked his fingers through his hair. "Come to think of it, she did make that one comment in the task force meeting . . . something about 'We're not a spa, we're a hospital.' I thought it was pretty heartless. Do you remember that?"

"Yes, I do," Patrick said. "I was hoping you caught it."

"And I was starting to hear things from docs at other hospitals who worked with her in the past. I confess, I didn't give them much weight."

Staci watched Patrick and Richard, wondering what was next.

"I wouldn't wish this on anyone, Richard, and this is probably not the right time—as I said. You know how I hate to classify people, but she was trouble, and she managed up very well. She put on one face with you and another with us. It's been brutal around here. I wouldn't put anything past her. I don't think she had a conscience."

"What are you saying?"

Patrick shook his head. "I'm not exactly sure. Something about this just doesn't feel right."

"Why didn't you talk to me?"

"You've been really busy. We knew you'd need lots of examples, and people were afraid to speak up . . . afraid of what she'd do to them. This is going to be messy. No one liked her—at our level at least—right, Staci?"

"Patrick, you can speak for all of us." Staci wanted nothing more than to stay out of it.

"Well, I've been blind. I need to think about how we'll handle this before everyone gets involved." Richard paused. Then he started thinking out loud. "I'm going to give Heather a call. But my gut tells me we should treat this as we would for any person who died of an apparent accident—probably a post, get security and HPD involved, talk with legal, and prepare for a press leak. I'm sure there's some organization we need to report this to, and before that, we need to find her family." He ran his hand through his hair and took off his glasses to polish them, thinking.

Staci found the courage to speak. "Human Resources should be able to help us find her emergency contact." Patrick nodded.

"I think Heather can access that information from home," Richard responded.

Staci hesitated to speak, but she knew she had to do it. Patrick had opened the door by telling Richard how bad things had been. She had to walk through it.

"I need to tell you both . . . something." She looked at the first and only men she had ever trusted. She could not find the words.

"What is it, Staci? You can talk to us," Patrick said.

She glanced down, then looked at Patrick and over to Richard. "I don't know how to say this . . . and you may not believe me . . . but I caught her trying to inject Mrs. Scalina with something."

"What do you mean?" Richard asked calmly.

Staci explained what had happened in Mrs. Scalina's room.

"You say you have the evidence?" Patrick asked.

"Yes, the wastebasket is still by her bed . . . My God! I hope housekeeping hasn't emptied it—let me run and get it."

"Go!" Richard said.

With relief, Staci ran from the scene in the stairwell. She took the stairs two at a time, dashed through the door, and headed to Mrs. Scalina's room. The wastebasket was where she had left it. Her heart hammered. She picked it up and returned to the stairwell.

"Here it is." Staci held the wastebasket out for them to see.

"When were you going to tell us?" Richard asked.

"Dr. Whiting, it just happened—minutes ago. I hadn't thought it through." Staci paused. "Honestly, I didn't know if you'd believe me. She told me you wouldn't. It would be my word against her word—she's management, I'm staff."

"Staci, I would have believed you." Patrick voice was firm with controlled anger and concern. "While my mind can't wrap around this right now—why she would do this—she was bad news. I bet if we dig deeper, we'll find even more disturbing information."

Staci just nodded. She was terrified. Digging deeper could discover even more secret bones.

"I'm going to call Dale Dawson in Security—he's former Secret Service. He's a good guy, and he'll know what to do." Richard pulled out his cell phone and scanned his directory. "He was a Marine sniper before he joined Secret Service. I occasionally go target shooting with him." Richard had zeroed in on the phone number. He looked up at Patrick and Staci. "We need to keep people out of here for a while. After I'm finished with Dale, I'm going to call Heather, then Elaine. Neither one of them like surprises." He shook his head. "But that's it, folks, for talking about this. Got it?"

Staci nodded, and Patrick took the lead, "Staci, take the CCU door, and don't let anyone in. Hang on to that wastebasket—you are the first in the chain of evidence. Don't let it out of your hands until someone with police authority asks you to sign it away. I'll go downstairs and stand at that door."

"Got it, Patrick."

Staci headed up the stairs, relieved to leave, clutching the wastebasket. She entered the CCU, stood by the door, and tried to slow her pounding heart. Would they discover that she had been in the stairwell with Sandra? She would cross that bridge when she came to it.

PATRICK

Patrick met Santos at the pub on Montrose for a late, casual light supper. He was grateful they had planned this date and he could see her in person. He needed to vent—and he was starving.

What a day! After finishing up with his patients and helping Richard manage Sandra's death, he was running really late, and he texted Santos to let her know. He would apologize and explain when he saw her.

He dashed through the door of the pub, and his eyes searched the room for her. The dark, peaceful pub, glowing with candles and fragrant with food, was a dramatic shift from the blazing lights, noise and intensity of the CCU. Immediately he started to decompress. He inhaled deeply. It smelled wonderful. The first thing to hit his nose was the scent of grilling lamb chops. Garlic permeated the air. Soft classical piano music played in the background. The lamps cast a gentle, soothing light on the wood and leather. Since it was a weeknight, the pub was nearly empty. Santos had snagged a booth tucked away in a quiet, dark corner. He was glad for that. What he had to tell her would have to be whispered.

She saw him and gave him a huge smile, then frowned. His heart was comforted that she sensed his mood before he could say a word.

"Hey, I'm really sorry I'm late." He leaned down to give her a quick kiss. She put her hands on either side of his face and searched deeply into his eyes. Then she closed hers and kissed him again. She held on, kissing him longer. Her lips were soft and warm with the taste of honey. He felt charged through and through with the energy of their love. Love restored. He was feeling better already.

"Maybe I should be late more often?" He smiled and slid into the booth, facing her. "I'm really sorry. I can explain. You know how I hate being late."

"You look exhausted. I've never seen you look this tired." Her eyes were full of love, concern, and questions. "Something must have happened. Let's get you something to drink. I just ordered us some grilled vegetables and cheese for an appetizer—I thought you'd be hungry because you're so late. You can start on that while you take a look at the menu, and then we can talk."

Gratitude for her flooded him. "I'll be fine. But I am starving. There was no chance to grab anything today. Hardly any of us even got a bathroom break."

"You worry me. This is more than the usual crazy day in CCU."

"Yes, it was . . . one of the most unusual days of my career."

"Okay, now you have to tell me."

The waiter brought their appetizer and two plates, took Patrick's drink order, and promised to return for their dinner choices.

"I don't even know how to begin," he started.

"It doesn't matter how it comes out. Just talk."

"Well, first, I think you're right that something's going on with Staci. She was very jumpy today—almost avoiding me. But that's not the real story."

He leaned forward, and she followed his lead, heads together so they could talk quietly. There was no way to escape it. "Sandra's dead."

"What?" Santos raised her voice, then sat back and

took a few breaths. She said quietly, "What happened?"

With the news out, Patrick sat back a little and wolfed down the food, explaining between bites how Sandra had been found in the stairwell, dead from an apparent fall.

"I wouldn't wish that on anyone," Santos said. "She was a toxic leader, and I wanted her off our unit, but not that way."

"We don't know if it was an accident—and I'm pretty sure it was, what with those heels she wore—vanity kills—but there will be an investigation. Though I agree that no one on the team would ever do anything as vicious as kill her, I ended up telling Richard a little bit about how she battered and abused the staff."

"What did he say?"

"He admitted to being totally blind. He knew bits and pieces but had chalked it up to gossip and discontent. But that's not the whole story."

"Okay . . ." Santos nodded her head and listened, then looked up and away from Patrick as the waiter appeared at their table with Patrick's drink. They gave him the rest of their order, and the waiter headed back to the kitchen.

"Coast is clear," she said.

Patrick took a sip of red wine and looked at her somberly. He kept his voice low. "Evidently, Staci caught Sandra trying to give Mrs. Scalina something IV push. Staci confronted her, and Sandra dumped the drug in the wastebasket."

"Do you have it?"

"Staci kept the wastebasket safe. It's being analyzed. I have no idea when we'll know more."

"What was going on?"

"Staci told us that Sandra said she was 'helping people along'—people on the Pathway who were meant to leave and go home or to hospice."

"You mean she was killing people."

Patrick nodded. "We'll never really know what happened. The only evidence we have is Staci's word and the drug in the wastebasket. We've lost two patients unexpectedly, but they *were* terminal. She could have drugged them in some way or ended their lives in another way, but I don't think there's any way we can track that."

"You're right, neither of them had posts. And she would know what drugs to use or how to make it look like a natural death. This is really serious, Patrick."

"I don't think it's over . . . my gut is telling me it's not."

"What do you mean?"

"The big question in my mind, and I hate to say this—is what happened between the time when Staci found Sandra trying to inject the drug and Sandra died in the stairwell?"

STACI

"I wish I knew the beauty
Of leaves falling.
To whom are we beautiful
As we go?"
David Ignatow

Staci tossed and turned all night. Anxiety trumped sleep.

Her fear was corrosive—little by little destroying her life. The life she had so carefully constructed. The illusion that had brought her joy, friendship, and meaningful work was vanishing. She had to get away from Blake before he found her again. She had to get away from the Medical Center before the police started to investigate her. Staci wished she believed in angels, as Santos did. Santos believed that angels watched over and protected people. There had been no angels in her life. Then she reconsidered, thinking of Patrick, Richard, and Santos. *Maybe I've just met my first angels?*

Sandra's discovery of the deception had been a near disaster, averted when she died. Though the death was awful, Staci felt little pity for her. Sandra getting what she deserved made Staci believe in karma more than ever. *What about my karma? What's to come of me?* And the patient deaths—would they ever be solved? *They were so innocent, so trusting. Everyone was trusting. They trusted me.*

Morning arrived, and her mind raced as she dressed for her last day at work.

I have to talk to someone. I have to get out of here.

She walked into the CCU early and noticed the conference room in use. Patient care would always go on, no matter what. *Pathways team meeting ... I missed it. Screwed up again.* Santos and Patrick sat together in the room, and Staci watched him smile so warmly at Santos that she blushed under his gaze. *They're so in love . . . so blessed.* She'd had no time to talk with Santos over the past few days as their shifts were different, and seeing her now stung deeply. *I'm really going to miss her . . . I lied to her. I lied to the person who has been the kindest to me in all my life.*

Melissa walked out of the meeting, cell phone at her ear. She nodded somberly and waved in greeting.

Staci waved but did not smile as she continued to walk down the hall.

Melissa was an attorney. What did they call it—attorney-client privilege? If she talked to her attorney, the attorney could not tell anyone. It would breach confidentiality. Santos trusted Melissa. Staci would too.

Staci turned around and walked back to Melissa, who was just finishing up her call.

"Melissa, could I ask a favor?"

"Sure, Staci . . . what do you need? We're kind of busy around here after yesterday."

"Yes, I know—I'm sorry to bother you now."

"Staci, you're never a bother," Melissa said, smiling kindly. "Just bad timing right now."

"I know. But I really need to talk with you for a while about something that's on my mind. I don't know who to talk to . . . and I thought maybe you? It's important."

Melissa took a deep breath and sighed. "Well, I've got a full day today, and you've got to work. But I have a medical staff meeting at six tonight. Why don't we meet right after that? I should be finished by the end of your shift.

Come over to my office. There won't be anyone in the suite, and the meeting will be private."

Staci found a smile and a glimmer of hope. Her breaking heart felt a bit lighter.

"Thank you, Melissa. I really appreciate this. I'm kind of at the end of my rope. I've got to talk to someone."

"I know. It's been wild around here recently . . . hard on everyone." Melissa reached over to gently grasp Staci's arm. She squeezed warmly. "Got to run now. I'll see you later. Okay?"

"Got it." Staci smiled and turned around to head for the lounge to put her things away. She had some homework to do before talking to Melissa. She would try to get it done during her short dinner break. Find a quiet place to think, compose her thoughts so she didn't sound like an idiot. She would tell her everything—about being an impostor, how Sandra had died in the stairwell, what Sandra had said to her before she died, and about Blake—and why she needed to leave. She needed time to wrap her brain around her confession. And she needed time to write a letter.

⤿

Staci was jumpy with anxiety and exhausted as she walked to Melissa's office. Her secret was an albatross that weighed more with every hour that passed.

She entered the small waiting area outside of Melissa's office. The windowless reception area looked like a small living room. Tastefully selected and conservatively upholstered chairs and a sofa were placed around a mahogany coffee table. Pictures of the Houston skyline hung on the walls. Green silk plants and an orchid added warmth to the room. It was quiet, as everyone had gone home for the day.

She put her bag and purse on one of the chairs. Too restless to sit, she paced the small space. She had prepared for the meeting as best she could. The letter was in her purse; the contents of her locker were stowed in the large bag.

Though she had worked side by side with Santos during the day, she had tried hard to mask her emotions. She played it very cool, professional, keeping Santos in the dark about her plans. Thank goodness they had been so busy their conversation was mostly limited to patient care, though Santos had asked her twice if everything was okay. She had to distance herself from the friendship that meant more to her than anything in the world. She had to rebuild the rock wall that would protect her heart from the pain of life. Yet she was deeply saddened knowing that she would never experience the joy of working and playing with such wonderful people again.

Talking to Melissa was a step she needed to take, but she was dreading it. It would bring some degree of closure to this chapter in her life—but it was a chapter she did not want to end. Her mouth was dry and her palms sweaty. *How will I find the words?*

Melissa walked in.

"Thanks for waiting." She smiled at Staci. "Long meeting tonight—lots of issues. But we're making progress."

"Thanks for agreeing to see me," Staci said as Melissa unlocked the door into her office. Her nerves were so frayed that she felt sick, and she suspected Melissa could see it on her face.

Melissa dropped her meeting materials on the desk and motioned for Staci to take a seat at the small conference table. Then she headed to a small refrigerator. "Want a bottle of water?"

"No, I'm good," Staci replied automatically and regretted it. She felt as if her mouth was full of ashes. She looked around the office at the diplomas and books, the awards, the symbols of a successful professional. All of a sudden, she felt her courage wane. Melissa was not just a colleague, she was a powerful leader. And Staci was about to tell her that she was a criminal.

"You know," Staci said, still standing, "maybe it's too late."

Melissa looked up at Staci and smiled. "Come on . . . you're worried about something. Maybe I can help." Melissa pulled out a chair and motioned for Staci to sit.

Staci sat down and dropped her head. She could not meet Melissa's eyes. This was a mistake. She was sure of that. She had to get out. But—

"Now we're not on the clock here," Melissa joked, "but I would like to get home sometime tonight." She laughed. "What's on your mind?"

Staci sighed and sat up straight, pushing her panic down. Now wasn't the time to run. She needed to do what she'd come here for. "I need to invoke—is that the right word? I need to invoke attorney-client privilege. What I say here has to stay here. I'm taking a huge risk, but someone needs to hear my story."

Melissa didn't speak for a moment. Her whole demeanor changed, and her warm blue eyes went cool and serious with the implications of Staci's request.

"Staci, I'm not sure what's going on here. But you're putting me in a very difficult situation. I think you know that. There's a lot at risk in a health-care setting, and keeping information quiet is not what we're about. We're about keeping patients safe. We really encourage people to come forward with the truth—even mistakes. If you've made a mistake, I can help you. But it needs to be acknowledged so we can do something about it. What you're asking me to do is to keep confidential whatever you tell me."

"It *is* about a mistake, but it's not clinical. It's personal." Staci paused to collect her thoughts. "I think once you hear my story, there will be some things you'll be able to do something about . . . things you need to know. There are other things you just can't talk about. So I guess, part of it is personal and part of it is about work."

Melissa sighed and sat back in her chair. She rubbed her temples as the implications drained her of energy. Melissa took a deep breath and made eye contact with Staci.

"Okay . . . talk to me."

Relief made Staci tremble for a moment, and she closed her eyes to get her composure back. The words flowed out in a torrential flood. "Oh, Melissa, I'm so sorry to do this to you, but someone has to know. I trust you. I know you will know the right thing to do. You're my only hope."

Melissa nodded somberly and motioned for Staci to begin.

"My name is not Staci Stevens. My first name is Staci, but I'm not going to tell you my real last name."

Staci spent an hour with Melissa, telling her story mingled with a few tears. She told her everything about being an impostor and why she'd done it. Staci told her about Sandra, the potential killings, and Blake. She explained that she'd meant no harm by taking on the role of a nurse—had no idea what she was getting into—how the whole experience had been enlightening and humbling and wonderful at the same time. Her organized plan fell by the wayside as her story gushed out to Melissa. She left out the deaths at the beginning of the story, but told her everything else. Living alone with a lie was a staggering load with heartbreaking consequences. She had kept so much inside over the past few months.

Melissa was respectful but firm. She told Staci that she'd given her a tremendous burden. Though she had listened without judgment, Melissa also expressed sadness at the choices Staci had made. Melissa reaffirmed Staci's plan of action to get out of the metro area, avoid contact with people who knew Blake, and seek a women's shelter, if she needed it, for the short term.

"Staci, you need to leave the hospital now," Melissa said, "and never come back."

Staci felt as if her heart was being ripped out of her chest. "Yes, I know."

"I need your ID badge." Melissa held out her hand.

Staci pulled the ID badge from her purse. She fingered the smooth surface one last time—this symbol of legitimacy, courage, and friendship. It was hard to give it up—harder than she'd anticipated. She put the badge in Melissa's waiting hand.

"Staci, for your own good, please don't give me any more information about your plans. This is the last time we can officially talk."

Staci nodded numbly. The gravity of her situation struck deeply. She was now completely alone.

Staci stood up to leave. There was nothing more to say. Melissa stayed seated and did not shake her hand.

Staci remembered the letter in her purse.

"Oh Melissa, one more favor, please." Melissa did not answer. "Would you please give this to Santos tomorrow? I am not going to be able to say good-bye. I don't know how to say good-bye."

Melissa nodded. Staci pulled out the letter and slid it

across the table to Melissa.

Staci dug in and found words one more time, "Thank you, Melissa. I'll never forget this kindness—I'm so sorry. I know I've disappointed you."

Staci saw sadness in Melissa's eyes, but Melissa did not stand up or reach out. Staci desperately wanted a hug, a loving, human touch—she was so lonely and afraid. But Melissa sat straight up and still. She finally dropped her head and looked down at the ID badge and the letter on the table. The silence between them lengthened. Staci gathered her things and walked to the door. She turned to look back at Melissa one more time.

"Melissa?"

Melissa looked up.

"Thank you," Staci said and walked away.

MELISSA

The office was so quiet she could hear the ticking of the clock.

When Staci left the room, her lips were quivering and her eyes were full of tears. Melissa desperately wanted to reach out, touch her, reassure her, but she couldn't. The steel boundaries of her professional role set limits on her humanity.

The walls of her office held the secrets of many serious and sad conversations. This had been one of the most difficult. She took a few deep breaths and reflected. Her emotions had run from surprise to disappointment to deep sadness. She had used every ounce of self-control to keep her face neutral and nonjudgmental as she listened. She wondered when or if anger would emerge. It usually did, but much later. She jotted down a few notes to help bring order to her thoughts. No one would ever see them. She had promised.

Her heart ached after hearing Staci's story, but she knew there was more. Women like Staci always had layers of backstory. Staci had just shared the essentials—the information that would soothe her conscience and get her safely out the door.

Melissa was deeply conflicted—torn inside about how she might be able to help a colleague, someone she had cared about, shared happy and sad times with, someone with whom she had worked with side by side. Yet that someone had committed a criminal act—at least one that she knew—there could be more. What other dark secrets lurked beneath the surface?

Was there anything she could ethically do? Her mind raced considering the possibilities.

The thought struck like a hammer and her fatigue vanished.

If Blake was as much of a threat as Staci thought, he could have tracked her to work. He could be on property. *Safety—I can give her safety—at least while she's on hospital grounds.* Melissa picked up the phone to call Security.

STACI

As Staci headed to the parking garage, she shook with the devastation of loss, as if someone very close to her had died. Tears blurred her vision as she walked to her car for the last time. She wasn't sure what she was going to do, but she had to go home and finish packing. Home . . . where would home be? Crushed with grief over losing her friends and her life, starting over with nothing, she walked numbly down the stairwell into the parking garage. *How could I have screwed up my life again?*

As she approached her car, she pressed the remote.

Blake stepped out from behind a pillar.

"Goin' somewhere, Darlin?"

Weary with life, she was almost too tired to register fear.

"Home . . . I'm going home. Shift is over. Got to get some sleep. Not now, Blake."

He didn't move. "We've got to talk, *now* . . . about us."

She found her voice and stood up tall. "There is no 'us,' Blake. There might have been a long time ago, but I'm not the same person anymore. I've got to go. I have nothing to say to you." Staci tossed her bags in the car and walked around Blake to the driver's side of the car.

He pulled out his Glock and pointed it at her. His face was stone cold.

"You'll find time for me now."

"Come on, Blake . . . don't—you don't want to do this."

"Nobody . . . but nobody . . . says no to me."

He'd obviously been drinking. His pitch-black eyes sparked lightning bolts of rage.

His voice shook with anger. "I could kill you right now . . . and no one would ever know."

Staci's heart pounded. She did not want to die—not on his terms. Adrenaline coursed through her body with every beat of her racing heart. She'd gone from exhausted to high alert. She felt naked without her gun.

She heard the stairwell door open and then bang shut—heard footsteps and voices.

Out of the corner of her eye, she saw Patrick and Santos enter the quiet garage. They were deep in conversation, holding hands and walking toward her. Blake stood with his back toward them. Hidden behind Blake, they could not see her. She was terrified for them.

Blake's Glock was leveled at his target—her chest.

She lifted her head and shouted over him, "Back off, guys!"

They stopped and saw her.

"Staci?" Santos called out.

Blake slowly turned his head, looking over his shoulder in the direction of Santos. His gun arm dropped to his side.

Staci had a second to act. She had to protect them . . . maybe even save herself.

She lunged forward, hoping to knock him off balance, simultaneously reaching for his gun arm.

He anticipated her move. His head swiveled back to face her, and she saw his mouth twist into a malicious sneer.

He fired . . . one . . . two shots. The bullets knocked her back, ripping into her abdomen, shredding tissue, creasing through blood vessels. "You bitch." He shot again. Pain twisted in her gut like a red-hot knife. She leaned over and watched the holes in her body run rivers of blood. Blood gurgled up her throat, her knees buckled, and she fell hard to the concrete. She heard footsteps, shouts, Santos and Patrick running toward her.

Blake stood over her. She looked at his well-worn cowboy boots, now spattered with her blood, and pulled herself up on her side. Blood was pooling on the concrete beneath her. Overcome by another sharp wave of pain that took her breath away, she doubled over, clutching her abdomen. She took a deep breath and looked up at him.

"Blake . . . please . . . don't."

He grinned sadistically and raised the gun one last time.

She ducked and flinched. Two rapidly fired shots reverberated loudly in the concrete garage. Blood splattered her, and bits of Blake's gray matter hit the pavement. His gun clattered to the floor and he fell within inches of her. In death, his cold, dull shark-like eyes stared at her.

Patrick ran up and kicked the gun away. "You got here just in time," he told someone outside of Staci's vision.

"I'll call in a Code Blue and 911 dispatch." Staci did not recognize the voice.

"Thanks, Dale," Patrick said.

"Melissa called me. She was worried he might be on property. Said he was dangerous. Good thing I was working another late night."

Staci's senses were on full alert from the pain-triggered endorphins that flooded her body.

Melissa called Security. She did understand. She did care.

Santos came into view. She dropped to the ground and

leaned over Staci. Santos yanked off her lab coat and rolled it into a ball.

"Oh, Staci . . . this is going to hurt . . . but I've got to put a lot of pressure on these wounds." Santos's eyes were full of tears. "Thank God Dale was here—Blake's dead, Staci—Blake's dead. You're safe. Hang in there."

"I'm so sorry, Santos . . . I'm so sorry. Please forgive me." The pain was so great Staci could hardly speak. Her vision was blurring.

"Sorry about what? This wasn't your fault."

"I don't have much time."

"You'll make it . . . hang in there . . . help is coming."

Patrick pulled Staci up into a sitting position, cradling her in his arms. It was easier to breathe this way. His body was warm. She felt sheltered. She could taste salty and metallic blood in her mouth. Santos continued to crush the now blood-soaked lab coat to the gunshot wounds, but Staci was starting to go numb. The pain wasn't so bad anymore.

She was cold and wet. She was breathing hard, drowning in her own blood. She knew she didn't have much time, but she had to do one more thing—one good thing.

She reached out, took Patrick's hand, and placed it on top of Santos's hands, slick with blood. "Promise me . . ." It was difficult to speak as blood pooled in her mouth.

"Promise you what, Staci? Don't talk, don't talk . . . save your energy."

Staci shook her head. She spit the blood out of her mouth and found her voice. "Promise me you will marry, have babies . . . make this world a better place because you . . . love each other."

She looked up at Santos, and Santos began to blur, and then get smaller and smaller. Suddenly Staci was falling, faster and faster down a dark, brick-lined tunnel. She was not afraid, just curious. She saw a pinpoint of bright white light. It drew her in. The light kept getting brighter and brighter, and she felt warm and safe. Tranquility surrounded her. An amazingly powerful and joyful energy drew her closer, as if a party of excited, loving friends waited for her. The blackness of the tunnel began to dance with tiny dots of bright light. The positive energy was potent and rich with happiness. The feeling of joy kept getting stronger. She could hardly wait to reach them.

She heard Patrick's voice, "We will, Staci."

"We love you, Staci," Santos's voice whispered.

Finally at peace, Staci closed her eyes and smiled.

"No man is of any use until he has dared everything."
Robert Louis Stevenson

Dear Santos,

When you get this letter, I'll have left town. I'm so sorry. I lied to you. I'm not who you think I am, and how I got into this mess, I'd rather you not know.

I'm not a nurse. When I first planned to take on the job of a nurse, I had no idea what I was getting into. I was naïve. I had no idea that it would be so hard, or that I would fall in love with the work, the patients, the team. I had no idea how complicated and painful it was—how every time you lose a patient, you lose a little of yourself—how the hole in your heart hurts—how fragile life is. Yet, the patients are always a part of you because you learned so much from them.

I was so careful with our patients. I studied their drugs, the doses, the interactions—so that I would not hurt them. I read every night till I fell asleep, journal articles and textbooks so that I might be accepted as a partner.

I'm not a monster. I'm not the same person I was when I started. I've been humbled by spending time with all of you. I lived in the shadows, on the dark side of the moon, and you showed me the sun. I feel that I lived life more in the few months that I was with the team than I lived in my entire life before. That I learned more than I ever dreamed possible. I felt welcome and warm—not lonely and on the run.

I felt loved for the first time in my life and that I was trusted. I betrayed that trust.

I don't know if I can ever fix what I've done, but I can't fix it here because deceiving you is the last thing I want to do. I've been lucky with patients, but I know I could kill someone. I need to go.

I was a runaway from my past. I hoped to be able to

leave it behind me and maybe make a difference, find another way. But my past has caught up with me, and I've got to go. Leaving you all—leaving the best time of my life—is the hardest thing I've ever done. But my conscience has finally come alive. What I did was wrong. As smart as I felt I was, I was not a nurse. I lied to the people I cared about.

I feel as if I've grown more in these past few months than I have in my entire life. I have found my moral compass. Now I need to use it to find the path away from this charade to something that's real.

You were the best, Santos. I ask that you forgive me. You gave me a tremendous gift—a glimpse into a life that I might have had if I'd made different choices. You showed me there was another way for a woman to make her way in this world—with strength and purpose and compassion . . . and hard work.

You and Patrick also showed me what real love looks like. It made me happy to watch you two, and so hopeful, that maybe someday I'll find someone who treats me with respect and loves me as much as Patrick loves you. And I'll love and respect him right back.

There is no way I can ever thank you. I hope you will remember the good things about me.

Good-bye. I love you.
Staci

PATRICK

"All of the most precious things in a human life are
the very things to which we find it most difficult
to make ourselves vulnerable and open."
David Whyte

Once again, he took her to Costa Brava Bistro, hoping to
rekindle the memories of happier times and move on from
the trauma—to heal. They sat opposite each other in the
cozy dining room, surrounded by oil paintings and bookcases lit by scores of small, flickering votive candles. The
warm saffron scent of paella and the smell of wood smoke
from the oven floated into the room.

They held hands across the small table. The only thing
between them was the soft light of a candle and a single red
rose. The darkness of the restaurant cloaked them in intimacy. Patrick thought he had never seen Santos so pale.
Dark shadows ringed her eyes, and a tear slipped silently
down her cheek. He reached over to stroke her face and
brush the tear away.

She smiled weakly at him. The light in her dark brown
eyes was dim with sadness.

"I can't believe she's gone. I can't believe she took the
risk of being a nurse impostor. I can't believe what we saw.
There is such violence in the world." She looked at him,
and her eyes sparked with outrage. "The world is so cruel."

"Sandra was on to her," Patrick replied. Richard and
Patrick had found Sandra's notes after her death. "She would
have been facing criminal charges for posing as a nurse."

"Sandra would have dragged her though the mud," Santos said bitterly. "And she would have enjoyed every moment of it." She paused, thinking. "Staci's past was going to catch up with her. It was just a matter of time. She risked everything—just for a chance to live another life. I guess she thought she had nothing to lose . . . she lost her life."

"They analyzed the specimen in the wastebasket. It was lidocaine. With Mrs. Scalina's heart block, it could have killed her. We're not sure how much was actually in the syringe—because there was paper in the basket that absorbed the drug—but in high enough doses, we both know it could have produced a stroke, or at least some severe neurologic consequences."

"So Sandra really had no conscience. Another sociopath—they look so normal most people wouldn't even know. I'm hoping, Patrick, that after our experiences we'll get better at spotting these kinds of people—recognizing that some of the behavior we see is mental illness."

Patrick squeezed her hands and looked at her, listening to her meandering train of thought as it switched back and forth between Staci and Sandra. It was good for her to let it out. He had no words that would console her. He had been talking with her for days now, and his heart felt the sharp edge of her pain.

Santos's eyes lit up. "Do really you think Sandra might have killed other patients before Staci caught her? We lost my favorite, Mrs. Cartwright, and then there was Mr. Hope-Simon. That's possible, isn't it?"

"It is possible . . . but I don't know how we would ever trace it. If Sandra did kill them, she knew how to cover her tracks—or make it look like someone else's mistake."

"She didn't want our Pathways plan to be a success—

did she? She wanted to sabotage our work—distract us—hurt us. She didn't care about us, about patients."

"No, she didn't," Patrick said somberly as he stroked her hand.

"Staci . . . she was a good person. She had a good heart. She *wanted* to do good. I know it!"

He nodded.

"Thank goodness she wrote that letter . . . otherwise we would have wondered forever why she took on the role of a nurse. I didn't like Staci at first. I thought she . . . wanted you." Santos stopped and looked at him. "That was really stupid on my part."

"No one could ever take me away from you, Santos. We're meant for each other."

Santos nodded, sobering again. "But I really grew to care about her. She tried so hard. She was humble, always asking for feedback." Santos paused to take a sip of wine. "Now I realize she was looking for reassurance." Patrick passed her his handkerchief, and she blew her nose.

"Her life must have been awful. She was so alone. She told me about her past, the foster care, how she spent so much time on the streets—how you and Dr. Whiting were the first men she ever trusted—in her life!" Santos looked at their hands on the table. "I can't imagine how my life would have been without my father. And she had no mother to count on either. But how could I be so blind not to see through her? What was I thinking?"

Her warm honey-brown eyes, shiny with tears, were full of questions, and her brow furrowed with frustration. He just waited, letting her talk it through.

"Patrick, I do believe what she said in the letter. I believe she did what she did—working with us—because she wanted to make a difference. I felt no malice in her. She tried so hard. She worked so hard."

"I agree. But what she did was really dangerous. She could have killed one of her patients—even though she didn't mean to."

"I know." Santos bowed her head, then looked up. "But she didn't. She didn't hurt anyone—except us. I'm disappointed in her actions, yet I miss her terribly."

Patrick reached over to stroke her cheek and nodded, swallowing a lump in his throat. He missed Staci, too. Though he had reservations about her, he had kept them to himself. He knew of women who had experienced the cruelty of abuse, but he'd never seen the pain and devastation it caused. Staci taught him more than he ever expected to learn.

He knew Santos's pain was deep with the sense of loss, and his heart ached.

"You've lost someone, someone you cared about. You're grieving."

He needed to move her to safer discussion territory. It was time.

"Santos, I believe she did make a difference. Let's talk about how ... let's remember her for what she did that was good. Most people aren't all black or white—they're gray. Though I believe there are evil souls, like Sandra, I don't believe Staci was one of them. Even if she entered our lives with a lie, she had goodness. God will judge her. It's not our place."

Santos smiled through her tears and nodded. "That's a good idea—to talk about the good things—to honor her brief life with us."

Patrick nodded and waited, reassuring with her with his eyes, glad his words were making a difference.

She smiled. "Well, she encouraged me to let go, to not

have such a huge need for control of my emotions. You know, this guy I dated once, a long time ago, told me he found me emotionally unavailable. Can you believe that?"

Patrick laughed, and Santos continued, "I probably was then . . . and as our friend David Whyte says, we must 'hazard ourselves and make ourselves available'—open to the world we want and need to experience. We might not have had Dos Brisas without Staci encouraging me to let go."

Santos paused and looked down. "The irony is—she'll never know we went."

Patrick nodded, and Santos continued to talk. He worked to keep his heart from leaping with hope at the direction she was taking the conversation. "It seems that David and Staci both believe that if we don't take risks—make ourselves open to the possibilities—the possibilities will never happen. You can't just open yourself to the good and filter out the bad."

Patrick smiled at her and saw her eyes begin to brighten. "I need to move on," Santos said. "Time to pull myself out this . . . I've got to get back to living my life—living with purpose—being more present for you—for us." She wiped her eyes and blew her nose. "See, it's a good thing I gave you handkerchiefs. They come in handy!" They both laughed.

Patrick suddenly remembered. "Oh, I meant to tell you. I heard from Elaine—who I ran into in the hall—that Emma is coming back. She'll be in charge until Heather returns."

"Well, thank God for that!" Santos replied. "Thank God!" She rearranged the silverware on the table. "You know, you're the only man I know who can generally see through women. Usually men are so blind . . . but you saw through Sandra."

"Well, she tried to win me over at first . . . she was quite the flirt."

"I never saw that! Really?"

"She rarely used her influence in public. She tried to find individual vulnerable points—then she used them to her advantage." He paused and looked gently at Santos. "I was already taken. She had no power over me."

Santos smiled back at him and squeezed his hand. "This is my lower self speaking, but do you know what Kamy said when she heard about Sandra?"

Patrick shook his head at the way the conversation was circling back. "Let me guess."

"Ding-dong the witch is dead!"

"I can hear Kamy saying that!"

Santos paused and looked around the room. It was quiet that evening, few tables occupied. "Patrick, what is the world coming to? Is there no safe place? No sacred place?" She looked at him as if he held all of the answers. He wished he did. "Is there no respect? Have we lost our conscience? The world, the workplace, has become so cruel."

He stroked her hand with his thumb. Her hands felt so small in his. He searched for the right words. "I don't know . . . about the world. I do believe that safe spaces, loving spaces, can be created. Life is full of trauma, violence, heartbreak—sadly, we live in a society that has sometimes lost its way, a world that is not always civilized."

She nodded and listened. His stomach began to churn with anxiety. This was the moment—the turning point. Was his timing right? He couldn't wait any longer. He chose his words carefully. He cradled both of her hands in his and spoke slowly and softly.

"Just as a home is built for shelter, so can a relationship with commitment create shelter, safety . . . peace. Though it has no walls, it can be stronger than place or time. It can weather the storms and trauma of life when two people decide to commit to one another and create a space where they stand stronger together than they stand alone. Think about it, Santos—we have known each other for a long time. We're both strong individuals. We'll always need to work on preventing burnout in our work. But that is easier with two people. We are committed to the same work. We understand what it takes and the struggles in the profession. But for me . . ."

He hesitated, then went for it. This was the most vulnerable he had ever been, but now was the time. He couldn't back down—he didn't *want* to back down. "I need a life partner in order to be complete. I need someone to grow with, have fun with, survive, and learn from life. I need you, forever."

Her dark eyes, glistening with tears, suddenly sparked to life with awareness. "What are you saying, Patrick?"

Patrick, always cool in a clinical crisis, felt overcome with shyness, uncertain of her response. He reached into his jacket pocket and pulled out a small red leather box. He opened it. A beautiful, round solitaire diamond ring sparkled against the black velvet lining. His heart was pounding with hope; his fingers wet with perspiration.

"It was my grandmother's. She would want you to have this. She would have really liked you."

He pushed it slowly and carefully across the table toward her.

Her eyes opened wide. She leaned forward and tentatively touched the box. Another tear slid down her cheek.

He couldn't read her. But he had to try. "I'm saying,

Santos, I love you. I've wanted you in my life from the first moment I saw you. I believe we have everything we need to create a safe place . . . a happy place . . . a marriage of equals. I need you to make me whole. I can't live without you. Santos Rosa, will you marry me?"

Santos looked down at the ring and shook her head slowly, thinking, processing. His heart fell. She was the love of his life. He had so many dreams he wanted to share.

"Santos, don't be afraid. I won't hurt you."

"Oh, Patrick, I just don't know . . ." Then she looked down at the rose and the candle, the ring of promise, all symbols of their future. She smiled down at them. He waited. His heart hammered, threatening to explode.

"Roses bloom amidst thorns—I think I read that in a poem or a book once," she said, fingering the stem of the rose. "Around anything beautiful, there is the potential for pain." She looked up at him and said, "I'm thinking. I'm thinking about what Staci told me one day, about how we can't control or schedule our futures, that we don't know when the time is right . . . or wrong."

She tilted her head to the side and smiled.

"Santos, tell me what you're thinking?" he asked gently.

"That you'll keep pestering me if I don't say yes."

Suddenly he felt hope. He could not help but smile.

"Yes, I will keep asking until you say yes."

She reached across the table for his hand and put it in both of hers. Her eyes were bright with love and happiness.

"You don't have to keep asking. Yes, Patrick. I love you so much. I'm not a fool. You're the best thing that ever happened to me. I need you. Yes, I *will* marry you."

He slid out of his chair, went down on his knees by her chair, and put his arms around her. They were eye to eye.

Her eyes were shining, and her face radiated happiness. He saw her love for him reflected in her eyes, and his filled with tears.

"I love you, Santos . . . I will never let you go." He brushed another tear from her cheek, touched the tip of her nose with his finger, and crushed her lips in a kiss. He tasted salty tears and sweet promise.

He took the ring from the box and slipped it on her ring finger. His heart was bursting with joy. The ring sparkled in the candlelight.

He gave her one more kiss, commingled with both of their tears, and left her side, sitting across the table from her. His heart pulsed with joy as he watched her admire the ring. It looked like it was made for her.

"I could look at this a million times in my life, and it would still make my heart leap with happiness." She turned to him and gave him a huge smile. Then she looked back at the ring and cocked her head to the side, thinking. He loved that look. He wanted to see it a million times. He would.

"What's on your mind?" he asked. "I can see those wheels turning."

"Patrick, have you noticed that since we've fallen in love, we've had some of the most 'interesting,' and I use that term loosely, experiences? I remember a book I read where one of the characters was labeled a trouble magnet. Are we trouble magnets? Just think about it. A cyber-killer, sociopaths, unsolved patient deaths, attempted murder, toxic leaders—an impostor, who we happened to love, who gets shot and dies in your arms. Need I go on? Is our life always going to be *this* interesting?"

Patrick smiled. "I don't know. We've had quite a ride so far. But I think, as long as we have each other, we have everything. Don't you?"

THE END

Thank you for reading this book.

If you liked it and even if you didn't, please consider posting a review on Amazon.

Reviews really help new authors.

For instructions on how to post a review, please turn the page.

Instructions for Posting a Review on Amazon

1. Sign in to Amazon using your email and password. If you don't have an account, it is easy to set up. Just create one using your email and add a password. You can't post a review if you don't have an account. You can do the same on Barnes & Noble.

2. Enter "The Impostor Triolo" in the search box. It will take you to the book.

3. If you've never written a review, just look at what other people have written. That may give you some ideas.

4. Click on the stars by the review. That will take you to a Review page.

5. Title the review, write it and submit.

That's all there is to it!

Thank you.

ACKNOWLEDGEMENTS

Though writing is a solitary creative craft, a book never comes together without a great deal of research, support and feedback. Before I thank those who helped create this new book, I want to thank all of the people who read and reviewed my first book, *Death Without Cause*. Thank you for spending your most precious resource—time— reading the book of a new author and writing a review. Your words guided and encouraged me.

I'm particularly grateful to the people who supported book signings, shared the book on social media, sent out e-mail blasts to clients and friends, gave away the books as gifts, invited me to book clubs, used the book in raffles and conference giveaways, and set up conferences and presentations. You hold a special place in my heart.

Writing fiction based in fact requires a great deal of research and study. References used in this book are located after the Acknowledgements. Thanks to the American Nurses Association for guidance about resources related to end-of-life care, in particular Laurie Badzek, Vicki Lachman, and Marla Weston.

I'm very grateful for the people from various walks of life and professional careers who agreed to be Beta Readers: William H. Dalehite, Jr., Katie Gibbs, Nancy Horton, Ann McKennis, and Cherie Triolo. Your feedback was invaluable.

The setting for this book is the Houston area. Though I could have created more fictitious sites, it was fun to include the names of some favorite local landmarks. Many thanks to Kitty Bailey and Angeles Duenas, the owners of

Costa Brava Bistro, Bellaire, TX; Brad Said for The Dosey Doe Big Barn, The Woodlands, TX; and Gillian Love of Lou Hammond & Associates for the Inn at Dos Brisas, Chappell Hill, TX for permission to use the names of these local establishments in this work of fiction.

My partners in publishing, Publisher Nancy Cleary of Wyatt-MacKenzie Publishing and editor and author Rachel Starr Thompson, take the written word, polish and present it. Nancy, you create the most professional products and finest covers ever! Rachel, keep that fine-toothed comb handy. You've taught me so much about expressing characters. Thank you both for your energy, wisdom, expertise and care.

And finally, and most importantly, this book would never have been born without the love and support of my beloved husband and best friend, Peter. Peter is my Alpha Reader. He tells me what I don't want to hear and then patiently waits until I hear it from the Beta Readers and Rachel. You're the best! I could not do this without you.

References can be found on the next page.

REFERENCES

American Nurses Association, http://www.nursing-world.org/mainmenucategories/ethicsstandards/end-of-life, 2014.

Barclay, Laurie. "End of Life Discussion Guide Aids Physician Planning," *Medscape Medical News*, accessed 8/26/2014 http://www.medscape.com/viewarticle/807827, 2013.

Csikszentmihalyi, Mihaly. *Flow: The Psychology of Optimal Experience.* New York, Harper Collins, 1990.

Kabat-Zinn, Jon. *Wherever You Go There You Are: Mindfulness Meditation in Everyday Life.* New York: Hyperion, 1994.

Gibran, Kahlil. *The Prophet.* New York: Alfred A. Knopf, 1976.

National Hospice and Palliative Care Organization, "NHPCO's Facts and Figures: Hospice Care in America, 2013 Edition," 2013.

Passino, Barbara. *Chocolate for Breakfast: Entertaining Menus to Start the Day with a Celebration from Napa Valley's Oak Knoll Inn.* New York: The Gerald and Marc Hoberman Collection, 2009.

Rubin, Harriet. *The Princess: Machiavelli for Women.* New York: Dell Publishing, 1997.

Teno, Joan M et al. "Change in End-of-Life Care for Medicare Beneficiaries: Site of Death, Place of Care and Health Care Transitions in 2000, 2005 and 2009." *JAMA* (309): 5, 2013.

Tzu, Sun. *The Art of War.* 6th Century B.C.

Whyte, David. *The Three Marriages: Reimagining Work, Self and Relationship.* New York: Riverhead Books, 2009.